DEATH
AT THE LAKE

Book 2

The Death Card Series

By

J.S. Peck

auSpeck

BEJEWELED PUBLISHING
LAS VEGAS, NEVADA

Bejeweled Publishing
6480 Annie Oakley Drive, Suite 513
Las Vegas, Nevada 89120

ISBN: 978-0-9824607-1-9
First Edition: September 2018

COVER ART DESIGN: Kelly A. Martin
INTERNAL DESIGN: Jake Naylor

DEDICATION

I dedicate the entire Death Card series to my talented sister, Judith Keim, who has taken time away from her successful authoring to help and support me.

"You have been the wind beneath my wings by believing in me and my talent for writing mysteries. When I've been in doubt, all I've had to do was pick up the phone, and you'd patiently share pieces of advice and encouragement. I honor and love you as my twin sister— I'm forever grateful."

CHARACTERS

B.B.	Signature on love note to Melissa
Brian Boyce	Investigator partner with Rosie/newsman
Bertha - "Mama"	Manager at Purple Passion Lounge
Cindy - "Sweet Thing"	Investigative partner with Brian and Mike
David Masterly	Manager of girls at Purple Passion Lounge
Gram	Rosie's grandmother in spirit
Jacklyn	Head of Agency for Human Trafficking
Jeff	MURDERED Rosie's fiancé
Johnny Cardoza	Manager with Tony at Purple Passion Lounge
Karen	Sister-friend
Lorenzo Mastrionni	Tony's go-fer person
Louie	Fashion Designer – friend of Romano
Maria	Safe-house mother
Melissa Johnson	MURDERED Dancer - Rosie's client
Mimi	Daughter of one of the owners of lounge
Mike Williams	Investigator partner/Rosie's fake boyfriend
Mrs. Givens	Mother of Melissa Johnson
Mrs. Wellborn	Sally's neighbor
Nancy	Sister-friend
Randy	Romano's life partner
Richard	Hairdresser suggested by Louie
Richard	Sophia's partner/owner PUP & lounge
Romano	Chef at Purple Passion Lounge
Ron and Irene	Rosie's neighbors
Rosalie Bennett	Tarot card reader – main character of series
Sally	MURDERED Dancer - Worked at lounge
Sam	MURDERED Worked at PUP
Steve	Employee of Brian and Mike
Susannah	Sister-friend
Sweet Pea	Rosie's dog given to her by her sister-friends
Sylvia	Bookkeeper at Purple Passion Lounge
Thomas	Employee of Brian and Mike
Tony Angelo	Manager/representative owner of lounge

TABLE OF CONTENTS

CHAPTER 1

As soon as I pushed through the door of my townhouse, I raced into the living room and threw myself down on the couch, Sweet Pea at my heels. I grabbed a pillow and screamed into it. I cried, laughed hysterically, and cried again, hard enough to cause hiccups. I was a total hot mess, exhilarated and exhausted. I was emotionally done.

I had to give credit to Sweet Pea, my darling silky dog, who sat at my feet. She never moved as she watched my antics. I think she knew I was in trouble - *big* trouble. I'd worked undercover at the Purple Passion Lounge to help solve the murders of one of my clients, whose tarot cards I'd read, and another dancer who performed there. Instead of nailing the murderers, I had participated in a drug bust and rescued four little girls the managers of the lounge had brought in to be sold in a human trafficking scheme.

Even now, all I had to do is close my eyes to see the four little girls staring back at me as they had when I'd unlocked one of the office doors and found them hiding inside. What was going to happen to them? What would happen to me for freeing them, which my old enemy the chief of police called kidnapping them? What about those people who'd love to get their hands on me for interfering with their plan? What was going to happen with the murders of my client and the other dancer yet to be solved?

Everything would have to wait; I couldn't worry about any of it now. I needed to get to bed and begin to recuperate. It was my turn to host my three best friends in Las Vegas in less than 24 hours, and nothing was going to keep me from that. Most important, for our safety, I couldn't let them know how much I was involved with all that was going on here with those murders. This was going to be hard to do because we usually have no secrets between us.

The next morning, I awoke feeling slightly better. As I lay in bed, I began to make a mental list of what I'd need to do before my friends got here, but before I could begin my plan, the doorbell rang, and Sweet Pea raced down the stairs to greet whoever was at the door. As I followed her, she barked with excitement and anticipation and wagged her tail.

When I opened the door, there was Brian, my investigative partner, who I was still working with to solve the murders, standing there with a worried look on his face. He looked so handsome, and I was attracted to him even though we seemed to be opposites. But the truth was neither one us wanted to be tied down at this point in our lives. We treasured the freedom to do what we wanted. That's the push-me-pull-you sort of relationship we had.

"Hi, there, Cowboy, what's up?"

Coming straight to the point, he asked, "Your friends are coming in today, right?"

"Not until tonight."

"Okay, that still works." He looked intently at me, a bit unsure of himself before he continued, "I've made arrangements for you and your friends, even Sweet Pea, to share a two-bedroom suite for the next three days at Loews out at Lake Las Vegas."

"Whoa, hold on." I shook my head in protest.

He immediately held up his hand and said, "It's on me. I've already paid for it all; it'll cost you nothing—meals and libation are included. Your being there will keep you safe and away from here until things settle down."

"Thanks, but no thanks. We're staying right here in my house. Besides, why would you do that?"

"We still have things to clean up, and I don't want you involved. The people we think are entangled in all the murders know where you live, remember?"

"Do you mean you have a lead on who killed Melissa and Sally?" I asked, my curiosity mounting. I didn't want to be left out of discovering and prosecuting the people responsible for my client's and the dancer's deaths. From the first, I vowed to do that, and I still wanted to be a part of it.

"We're working on it, but there's no room for you to be involved," he repeated emphatically before throwing in the last incentive, "Besides, the last thing you want to do is get your girlfriends hurt, right?"

He had me there. I hated to give in, but I could see his point. "If I agree, I don't want you to pay for anything. I'll take care of it myself."

"Too bad; it's already done. You can pay for the other things you girls do, though."

"I've already purchased tickets to see a show at The Smith Center one of the nights …"

"No problem," he immediately cut in. "I'll have a limo pick you up. Just let me know which day and time."

"Just how are you managing to do all this, if you don't mind my asking?"

"Well, I *do* mind," he said firmly, dismissing any chance of a response. "Just promise me that you'll leave first thing in the morning, Rosie. Enjoy it out there."

As I hesitated, he added, "You deserve a break from all this. Get a massage or a—what do you girls call it—a 'mani-pedi'—or something? Just *stay there* and have *fun*."

I stood in front of him, weighing the pros and cons. He interrupted my train of thought by adding, "I'll have security there for you too. But if anything comes up or you need me, call me right away. Just go and enjoy," he insisted.

Hmmm. Although I wasn't feeling entirely comfortable about his proposition, maybe this wouldn't be such a bad idea after all. I was more than a little worried I might have more unwelcome visitors here at the house while the girls were with me. I certainly didn't want them to become involved or get hurt.

"Well? Promise me?" He paused. "Just tell them you won a prize or something," he coached.

"Okay, deal," I said reluctantly as we shook hands. Then he pulled me forward, looked deep into my eyes, and gave me a kiss on the forehead. What's up with that? I wondered, especially after he'd given me a passionate kiss when he'd helped to save me and the little girls.

He bent down to pat Sweet Pea before he turned to leave. "I've paid the guard at the gate to keep a careful watch over your house tonight and for the next few days. Call me if anything more happens—I mean it."

Death at the Lake

I stood there but didn't know what to say, so I said nothing as he walked out the door. I wasn't used to all this concern or relying on someone else. Sometimes it made me feel as if I were floating along, doing what anyone wanted me to do, but I didn't have a choice. Maybe this time I didn't.

I looked at the clock and realized I now would have to redo my shopping list to buy treats—sunscreen, beach towels, and more—to take to Lake Las Vegas. I would also have to pack for Sweet Pea, who'd be overjoyed and excited about joining us. She loved staying at hotels and acting as the official greeter whether or not anyone wanted her to be. Luckily, she was cute enough to get away with it.

The day sped by, and before I knew it, it was time to pick up my "sister-friends" at the airport. They had managed their flight times so they landed just about 20 minutes apart, making it easy for everyone to gather there before we headed to my house together.

My sister-friends (more like sisters than friends) and I always had fun together, doing whatever inspired us at the time. We never knew what was going to happen, which made it even more crazy fun. I was lucky enough to attend Cornell College, where I met and befriended these three fabulous women—two from Boston, Massachusetts, and one from Boise, Idaho. They are the ones who'd alleviated the pain of my having been belittled and bullied for my and my grandmother's psychic abilities when I was younger.

I loved my girlfriends, for they filled my life in ways so wonderful it was hard to describe. I couldn't wait to see them.

First to arrive was Nancy from Boise. At first, she was hard to find in the crowd because she is petite, only 5 feet tall. It was her wild, blond, curly hair I saw between taller people that made me able to grab her from the line and hug her. My 5'10" dwarfed her, but her smile was huge and electrifying, making me so grateful she was my friend. Nancy was the "tomboy" who loved all sports and animals. She even owned four nonallergenic dogs of her own. At college, she took courses to become a veterinarian, but her allergies to animals kept her from actually working with them on a daily basis. Instead, she worked from home for the offices of an organization that raises funds to protect endangered animals around the globe. She loved her job and traveled around the world to see some of these animals herself—always taking her allergy medicine along.

We chatted away while we waited for Karen and Susannah to arrive. Nancy showed me pictures of her newest puppy and videos of all four of her dogs playing together. They were hysterical.

Then we heard a tremendous shout—"Helloooo."—so we knew Karen had arrived. She was the unrestrained "kid" who found fun in almost everything she did. She taught first grade—no surprise—and had won several awards for her way with children, and her ability to help international students settle into America and the English language. She danced her way toward us, waving her arms in the air above her head. "I'm so glad to be here, ladies. We're going to have so much fun together."

We exchanged hugs and kisses, and then Susannah showed up, looking as trim and professional as could be. She was the "perfectionist" and always wanted everything to be in order. Susannah had a rough childhood living in the ghetto, and had a bit of a control issue, but she knew it about herself and was able to laugh at her ways. A corporate lawyer in Boston's financial district, she dressed and looked the part in all the best ways. Other people often found Susannah intimidating, but we three didn't. Susannah could be a hoot, for she had a very dry sense of humor. We loved to be in her company.

After collecting our things, we drove to my house. "So, what's happening, Rosie? Anything exciting?" asked Nancy as we entered the house.

I remained silent, since Sweet Pea was rushing forward, barking her pleasure at seeing the girls. She was convinced, I think, they'd come just for her. She was their gift to me after my fiancé, Jeff, died, and everyone loved her and treated her like one of the girls. Because Sweet Pea is nonallergenic, Nancy immediately swooped her up in her arms and received many kisses for doing so. The other girls pampered her as well. She looked up at me with a huge smile. It had taken me time when I first had her to realize that yes, indeed, dogs really can smile.

"Hold on, girls. Don't unpack your bags yet ..."

"Woo-hoo." Karen cried out. "A surprise. I knew you were up to something special when we talked the other night—I could hear it in your voice."

"Well, I do have a surprise for us all. We were given a two-bedroom suite at Loews for the next three days at Lake Las Vegas. We head out tomorrow. Even Sweet Pea is invited," I added.

"Woo-hoo," hollered Nancy. "I love that place. Isn't that the same one we drove out to see and where we had cocktails the last time we were here?

"It sure is," answered Karen. "I wouldn't forget a place like that."

"Ladies, let's go upstairs," I said. "Your presents for this trip are in the first guest room."

"Wow, more surprises?" asked Karen.

"Are you sure you want to spend your money like this?" whispered Susannah in an aside to me. She was my lawyer and handled most of my financial affairs and my trust fund. She asked me despite knowing I have more than enough money to do that and anything else I wanted, thanks to my parents and Grandmother's keen investment sense.

"Our time at Lake Las Vegas is a thank-you for doing a favor for a special client," I informed them. "Room and board are on the house; all else is on us. Not bad, huh?" I hated not telling the whole truth, much less calling Brian a client.

"I'll say. I sure would love to meet this client of yours," enthused Karen.

"You never know ..." I responded in a low voice.

Excited as little girls, we all scurried up the stairs and piled into the first guest room. Four bundles, alike except for the color of the beach towels, were on the bed. "Just pick one, and I'll take what's left," I directed.

Each of the girls grabbed a pack, and we ended up laughing because we all were comparing what we had with what the others had – like old times at college.

"Let's head downstairs for a nightcap before we go to bed," I suggested. "How does Amaretto on the rocks sound?"

Karen said, "Now we're talking." She wasn't a real drinker but loved to indulge with the rest of us.

Nancy and Susannah chimed in together, "Count me in."

We settled in for just a short session of small talk before heading back upstairs to bed. Tomorrow at Lake Las Vegas would be the real start of our sister-friends weekend, and we couldn't wait for it to begin.

CHAPTER 2

I t was just 8 o'clock when the girls came down-stairs, dressed for the day, packed and ready to go. After each of us had a quick cup of coffee, a piece of fruit, and a freshly-baked croissant, we loaded up and piled into my SUV to drive out to Loews. Brian had made special arrangements for us to check in early, and we were ready for fun, sun, and water.

It had been quite a while since my last visit to Lake Las Vegas, and the area had changed, particularly because the main casino in the village had sold and now stood empty. For all its beauty and glorious houses with Italian flair, Lake Las Vegas was suffering lack of traffic and economic support. But it was on its way back, and I'd always believed it would become more economically sound in the near future. With the hotels already there and more and more visitors coming to the Las Vegas area looking for places beyond the Strip, Lake Las Vegas would certainly become the place to visit, or even live.

We drove through the main entrance with its tall palm trees and passed the waterfalls, where many brides have their photos taken, and traveled along the curving road that cut through the gorgeous golf course, with manicured grass on both sides of the road. As we reached an incline near the clubhouse, we had a full view of the Strip down in the valley below. I loved Las Vegas and its vast valley with all its different aspects, especially its wide-open space, where you can see for miles. We continued driving past the village, which still held several wonderful restaurants and a few shops. Then we drove to the end of the road, and there was Loews with its fancy driveway and welcoming large pots of tropical plants.

As we were slowed down, Sweet Pea stood on Nancy's lap and looked out in anticipation of what lay ahead. We all stretched toward the windows, and I felt the girls' excitement build. This was going to be a wonderful break for all of us, I thought with pleasure.

After checking in and receiving the dog dish and mat they were famous for handing out to their canine visitors, we headed to the suite. It was large, with two adjoining rooms, each with a bathroom and bedroom area and two queen beds. In between the two bedroom areas were the kitchen/dining area and a rather small but comfortable living room, great for reading or watching television. Perfect.

We hurriedly unpacked, and then we all raced down to the front of the resort and out onto the large outdoor patio, where couches and comfy chairs were scattered about a large fire pit and a decorative fountain area in the center. The patio had tiers of steps leading down onto a path that meandered around the lake. Just being there at Lake Las Vegas made us feel as if we were in a different country. I knew being there would be renewing for all of us.

"Look," shouted Karen, "paddle boats. Let's go."

I grabbed Sweet Pea and ran down to hop into one of them with Nancy. "Come on, Sweet Pea," Nancy shouted, "c'mon with me. There's space for you right here beside me."

Luckily, it was one of those perfect days—warm but not too warm—so we didn't need to worry about the sun burning us just yet.

Afterward, we changed into our swimsuits, plopped on our new hats, and carried our gift bags to the small beach by the pool. Later we'd take our swim in the pool; the lake wasn't clean enough. Sweet Pea wasn't a worry because she was content back in the room, snuggled on my bed.

We lounged in the beach chairs for a while until Nancy suddenly jumped up, saying "I can't wait any longer. It's time to eat." It was always fun to watch Nancy eat, for she enthused over everything and could really pack it away. She was the smallest of us but always ate the most.

Susannah looked at her watch and said, "You've got to be kidding—it's only 11 o'clock." She was not as flexible as the rest of us and was used to doing things on a tight schedule. Suddenly, she sprang up from her chair and laughingly said, "What the hell, why not? We're on vacation."

Karen and I looked at each other and smiled. We were all so predictable. Karen and I first met the day we literally bumped into each other as we lugged our things into the room the college had assigned us as roommates. We hit it off from the very beginning and remained close friends ever since. As our freshmen year progressed, we met

Nancy and Susannah, who lived on the same floor, just down the hall. We began to hang out together, and by our sophomore year, we requested a four-person suite, where we lived for the rest of our time at Cornell.

In reality, it was sometimes hard to believe that we could be such close friends, because we couldn't be more different. Yet, just like close siblings, we were always there for each other and truly loved each other in wonderful, healthy ways.

I tended to be very private, wrapped up in my own thoughts, just as I had been as a little girl. My friends helped me come to value who I was and what I offered as an intuitive and a writer, which gave me the freedom to enjoy life as I saw it. Gram always said the girls gave me wings, and I believed that's true.

As I began to open up more to the enjoyment of friends and things outside myself, I fell madly in love with Jeff. He was the policeman who stopped me for speeding one night as I was driving home after an evening with the girls. Soon he was the topic of conversation each time we had a group telephone call. It was they who encouraged me to step outside my shell and embrace the good fortune of Jeff and my finding each other. It was also the girls who were there to help me pick up the pieces after the devastating ordeal of Jeff's death and all the things he had been falsely accused of doing, and had become the fall guy for the drug dealing that happened in his department. Gram had passed by then, and I didn't know what I would've done without my three beautiful friends. That was three years ago, but it seemed more like three lifetimes ago.

"C'mon, Rosie, stop daydreaming. Let's eat," called Nancy, who led us through the resort to the little outside restaurant beside a small garden. We sat on the patio for lunch and listened to the palm trees rustle each time a warm breeze blew. It was heavenly. We each ordered their special sandwich—their "slim" choice, made with tomatoes, avocado, sprouts, and a mayonnaise/mustard sauce on multigrain bread. It was delicious, but then we spoiled all that slimness by eating their specialty—key lime pie. This was part of the being "naughty" that Karen referred to each time the four of us gathered, for it was she who was always watching her weight.

Before long, the warm weather and food got the best of us. "Let's go back to the suite and regroup for an hour or so," suggested Susannah.

We headed back to our suite to lie down, relax, or read, though I decided to take Sweet Pea for a walk around the lake instead. I was too keyed up thinking about all that'd happened during the previous weeks, as I knew it wasn't over yet. Although Brian, Mike, and I were determined to discover who'd caused both Melissa's and Sally's deaths, we hadn't yet addressed Sam's murder, which had been reported as a robbery. We knew it wasn't, though, because his wallet was found by his side with all his money intact. I believed all three murders were connected to one person, although the guys weren't convinced of that yet. There definitely was more trouble headed our way, and I needed to remain calm and open to any psychic messages coming to me. Other than meditating, the best way for me to do that was to take a walk.

As Sweet Pea and I began to start down the path around the lake, a feeling of foreboding overcame me, and I felt a little sick. Refusing to move farther down the path, I pulled Sweet Pea off the path and let her do her thing where we were. I immediately relaxed when a breeze ruffled my hair because I knew it was Gram visiting me. *"Hi, Sweetheart.*

Glad the girls are with you. Enjoy them, but be careful. Love you."

Afterward, I headed back to the suite and was greeted by Karen, who was waiting for me. "Time to do the cards, Rosie. I need some answers."

Because of all that'd happened recently, I wasn't sure I wanted to know what was likely to happen to any of us, but I relented. "Okay, give me a few minutes to quiet my mind, and then I'll get them."

The reading was very accurate with regard to what I knew to be true for Karen in the past. The present was filled with cards expressing friendship, hardships overturned, and travel ahead for her. The future was filled with a lover (maybe two), more travel, and the marriage card, which made her a bit nervous. The last card, the outcome, was the World card—the best card in the deck as far as I was concerned—representing success. It was a wonderful reading for her, and I was glad. She deserved happiness and true love in her life at last.

Susannah and Nancy rolled out of bed. "We want readings too."

I wasn't in the mood for full readings because my mind was still wandering, filled with worry, so instead, we sat in a circle, and everyone picked a card for the day. Karen's was the Five of Cups, meaning *"Don't run away from your feelings. You have been waiting for this new beginning for a long time."*

Nancy's was the Ace of Pentacles, with its meaning *"Get your talents rolling. Do your own thing."*

Susannah's was the Three of Cups—*"Don't be afraid of emotional reactions. Open up to others, or make your limits plain."*

Mine was the Eight of Wands, which told me *"Great tasks require great efforts—in this case, more intuition and awareness."*

Then it was game on, for as we had always done in the past, we took the meaning of our card and told the others something that was going on in our life that related to it. That was our philosophical time, and it usually was extremely interesting and thought-provoking.

Karen, of course, wanted to go first, for she was excited about sharing her news, and rightfully so. "Okay, here it goes. You know how I've not been interested in a man for a long time, right? Well, guess what? I've just met someone. I swear he's the love of my life, maybe even my soul mate."

The rest of us paused and remained silent for a long time before we showed any excitement, and she responded, "I know what you're thinking; you're remembering my time in college with that weirdo. It's nothing like that. He's the brother of one of the teachers I work with, and he's also a teacher. You'll like him, believe me. Before you even ask, here's his name so you can Google him for yourself," she added smugly, knowing we'd definitely do that. We laughed and asked more questions about this new person in her life until it was time for Nancy to share.

Nancy was also enthused about taking her turn. "The meaning of my card couldn't be more perfect either. As you know, I've been working for the same nonprofit for years, bringing in funds to help save some of the endangered animals around the world. It has become increasingly frustrating because I know that I'm their top person responsible for bringing in the largest share of donations, yet they aren't even addressing some of the causes I've championed, so I've been talking to some of my donors from the past to see whether they'd support me if

I set up my own nonprofit. That way, I can specialize in saving the elephants and the South African penguins. And guess what? They are encouraging me to do it, and they've promised me financial support."

We all agreed that Nancy would be the perfect person to take this on. We all loved animals, so we were excited to discuss some of the ways she could market her nonprofit. Of course, Susannah volunteered to be Nancy's attorney, even though that was not her field of expertise; Karen said she'd have her kids paint pictures of the animals for advertising purposes; and I volunteered readings to guide her along the way.

Susannah sat quietly, but a smile was tucked in the corner of her mouth. It was her turn, and we looked at her expectantly. She sat there silently until we pushed her to take the opportunity to talk about her card. "You all are going to think I'm just a silly woman with no real meaningful priorities in life," she said.

"What are you talking about, Susannah?" I exclaimed. "That's not you."

"I agree," chimed in Karen.

"Just let her talk," encouraged Nancy. "Go ahead, Susannah."

"All right. Most women our age are looking forward to having children and eventually grandchildren. You already know that Henry and I decided not to become parents, right?" Then, with her smile spreading across her brown face, she continued. "However, we've decided to become a more complete family by purchasing two Silky terrier puppies from a breeder in Connecticut. We're going to pick them up in a week or so." She asked excitedly, "Do you want to see their pictures?"

We all clamored around to see pictures of her babies and shouted and yelled different suggestions for names— one male and one female. Chanel seemed to be the winner for the girl and Brut for the boy. But any suggestions had to be approved by Hank, so nothing definite could be decided right now. "Okay, Rosie, it's your turn now," Susannah prompted me.

I was nervous about sharing. I didn't exactly know how much to divulge although the message—*"Great tasks require great efforts – in this case, more intuition and awareness"* seemed appropriate in more ways than one. I already knew I seriously needed to step up my awareness and use my intuition more, and the message from this card only confirmed it, so I began my story.

Of course, I left out some of the grittier details of my experiences. I didn't want to cause the girls to worry about me. Still, there was much to share. I began telling my story at such a fast pace and tried to get it over with in such a hurry that Susannah exclaimed, "Whoa, hold on. You mean to tell us that you're involved in two murders?"

"Well, not exactly," I stalled. "I'm just collecting information for my new column at *Women Living Well* on "What's Hip in Las Vegas," and I'm helping Brian so that he can apprehend the killer and ..."

"Just who is this Brian?" asked Nancy, cutting in.

"What do you really know about him?" asked Susannah, wearing her lawyer frown.

"I'm going to Google him," Nancy threw into the conversation, as she rose to grab her iPad.

"Hold on, let's finish this conversation first," ordered Susannah. "You've been working at the Purple Passion Lounge as an undercover agent? And you're still involved with the murders? I don't like this one bit, Rosie."

"I agree," chimed in both Nancy and Karen.

I was very aware they didn't approve of my involvement, and there also was Brian's demand that I opt out. Even if the Purple Passion Lounge closed after all that had happened and I no longer worked there, I still intended—with or without Brian and Mike—to find out who murdered Melissa and Sally. "Now, my dear friends," I said in a calm, determined voice, "You are just going to have to trust me on this. I promise that if things begin to get out of line, I will end it and step away from all of it."

"That might not be as easy as you think; I wish you would step away right *now*," Susannah said, with disapproval written all over her face.

Karen piped up in a soothing voice. "Although we may not like it, we need to allow Rosie to do what she wants. She'll know when the time is right time for her to step away and end it."

"You're right," Nancy agreed, reluctantly. "It's not like Rosie can't handle herself. But you have to promise us, Rosie, that if you need our help, you'll let us know, okay?"

Relief flooded through me as they let me off the hook, but it didn't stop the worry building inside me. I knew at this point I needed to be more alert than ever, as it would be important for me to be able to pick out anything the least bit out of the ordinary happening around me. Things weren't right, and I needed to be extra careful. In addition, I now had the worry of keeping my friends safe as well.

CHAPTER 3

II What time is it?" asked Nancy.

"If you say it's time to eat, I'm going to scream," teased Susannah.

"Not eat," responded Nancy with a grin. "Time for a mojito on the patio."

"Sounds great," we all cried in unison. As we got to our feet, I was glad to be moving on to something more carefree. I gathered up the tarot cards and saw the Death card sticking out. I shoved it back into the middle of the deck and joined the girls, who had already grabbed their bags to go to the patio. I reached for mine and called to Sweet Pea to join us.

Once outside, I could tell that I needed to walk Sweet Pea again, so I called to the girls, "Save me a seat, and order a mojito for me."

As I followed the path along the lake, I could sense rather than hear someone coming down the path behind us. I didn't want to be found there alone, so I picked up Sweet Pea and tucked her under my arm. Then I stepped off the trail behind a clump of beautiful purple-flowered bushes that were thick enough to hide us, and I bent low. Sensing my worry, Sweet Pea stayed quiet and remained so as a man walked by. After he had taken a few steps away from where we stood, I peeked out to see if it was someone I recognized. My breath caught, and my heart fell. He looked like the second man who had broken into my house. I'd already had a confrontation with his sidekick a few days ago, and I didn't want a repeat performance. It definitely was time to call Brian. After all, he was the lead on the murder cases, the person I was supposed to call for anything related to the investigation.

When I punched in his number, his phone rang and rang with no response, which left me no choice but to leave a message. "Hey, Cowboy, give me a call, please."

I expected him to call me back right away, but my phone remained silent for the rest of the day. Something was up, for sure, something bigger than my incident, or he'd have certainly called me by now, wouldn't he?

Later, as I changed into my evening clothes and got ready to drive the girls into the village for dinner, Sweet Pea sat on the bed and watched my every move. I mumbled to her, "What's going on, Sweet Pea?" She just stared at me intently.

We were looking forward to going to the small village on the other side of the lake. It had narrow, cobbled streets winding around the few stores, galleries, restaurants, and two hotels. It's quite charming and would make a nice evening away from Loews.

Death at the Lake

As we walked down the sloping hill toward the water—the same lake that surrounds Loews—I pointed out the charming, small condos with beautiful lake views that were above a section of the stores. We continued farther down the hill to my favorite store, which sold many fascinating items from Mexico. The girls really wanted to shop, and they bought a few mementos of the "wild, wild, West" before we headed to the only Mexican restaurant there. It was perfect weather, and we sat outside on the large patio with an expansive view of the lake. It was time for me to let worry go and enjoy being with my friends.

"Do you all want a frozen margarita?" asked Nancy. "My treat."

After we each ordered and the waiter left, we sat munching on the tortilla chips and salsa he'd provided. Then, after the waiter handed us our cold drinks, we toasted each other. When it was my turn to raise my glass and give a toast, I spoke from my heart. "Here's to my beautiful friends. I love you all," I proclaimed as my eyes teared up. "You're the best."

"Amen," all three said in unison, and we smiled at the luxury of being special friends. I was beginning to unwind and relax on this beautiful evening, and it felt good. We perused the menu, and each of us ordered something different. We decided to have an assortment of things to nibble on, not caring about whether they were healthy: beef empanadas, carne asada fries, ceviche, Mexican pizza, and, of course, nachos. Nancy, more than any of the rest of us, was in seventh heaven. For her size, it was *amazing* that she could eat so much and still remain toned and slim.

As we continued to sit, eat, chat, and laugh, I felt the hairs on the back of my neck stand straight up. I paused, trying to figure out what was causing this reaction, and then I heard Sophia's boss and former business partner speaking behind me. Sophia had been my supervisor at a ride-sharing service—PUP, which stood for Pick Up. I'd worked there for a few days before I started at the Purple Passion Lounge as an uncover agent working for Brian.

I whipped around to see him lean over and speak to a couple seated two tables away. He'd frightened me when Sophia died, and I wanted nothing to do with him; in fact, I wanted to get as far away from him as possible. The other girls didn't seem to notice my reaction, and I tried to act casual when I rose. I grabbed my purse and said, "I'm off to make a bathroom run. Be right back."

They nodded and Susannah added, "Hurry back, we don't want you to miss anything."

I'd held back from mentioning to the girls all that'd happened at PUP during the few days I'd worked there. Sophia's boss, Richard, had threatened my life if I told anyone about Sophia's sudden death of a heart attack. Simply by his being a part-owner of the Purple Passion Lounge connected him to the two murders Brian and I were trying to solve, and Richard didn't want to raise any more suspicion about any of his suspected involvement with the deaths of the two strippers. I still felt vulnerable to this man, who was now on the patio with me.

Seeing him brought back the vision I'd had at the time of Sally's murder. I saw him push wildly through the crowd that'd gathered there, and he'd acted distressed when he saw Sally was dead. He'd frightened me then, and he certainly was no one I wanted to deal with in any way, particularly not now with my friends here.

The bathroom was in an odd location. It almost seemed an afterthought, tucked at the end of a long hallway and accessible only after a last-minute turn. It was certainly not a safe area, and I felt prickles along my arms as I neared it. When I turned to enter, someone came up to me from behind and covered my mouth with his hand. I was paralyzed with fear. He whispered, "Don't make a sound."

When I recognized the voice, I was filled with anger and mortification at being attacked like that. "Cowboy, if you ever do that to me again, I'll ..."

"I couldn't take a chance that you'd scream. What the hell are you doing here, anyway? The deal was that you would stay at Loews."

"I didn't realize that meant we couldn't go to the village. Just what are *you* doing *here*? And why didn't you call me back after I left you a message?"

"I'm sorry about that, really I am. We've been tailing your PUP boss from town, hoping he'd lead us to the big boss, but we lost track of him. I was hoping he'd show up here."

"Well, you're in luck. I just saw him out on the patio—but that's not why I called you. When I was walking along the path around the lake at the resort, I was followed. I hid behind some bushes beside the path, and I recognized the man when he walked by. I'm pretty sure he was one of the guys who broke into my house."

Brian frowned. "Well, it seems we've trouble everywhere at the moment, and you're not safe. Listen to me, Rosie, I want no bullshit argument from you, understand? You *have* to return to Loews right now. I mean it."

When he saw I was resisting, he coaxed, "You'll be safe there. I've stationed someone there to protect all of you. His name's Steve. He's middle-aged, rather average-looking, and someone you'll recognize because he'll be wearing a Boston Red Sox baseball cap."

As it was beginning to sink in that I had to do everything I could to keep the girls safe, Brian tried to lighten the mood, "Just don't tell Steve I said he's average-looking, okay? He's sensitive about that."

I stared at Brian, knowing his intentions were good, but I wondered whether anyone could keep us completely safe. Worry filled me, and I became lost in thought. When I realized that Brian was watching me closely, my stomach began to flutter. He bent toward me and locked eyes with me, and we stood staring at each other, never moving. Neither of us had a clear understanding of how we stood on a romantic level after the passionate kiss we'd shared when he'd rescued me and the four little girls. Then he sighed and simply kissed me on the forehead instead of repeating a more intimate kiss. He stepped back, pushed me toward the restaurant, and said in a hoarse voice, "Now get out of here."

When I reentered the main restaurant area, I located our waiter and called him over so I could pay our bill before joining the girls. I peered around to see whether I could locate Sophia's partner. I didn't find him but soon heard his voice in the bar behind me, fortunately where he was out of sight.

I was relieved not to have to deal with him and pasted a pleasant smile on my face as I approached the table where the girls were waiting for me. "Time for nightcaps on the Loews patio, ladies."

"Where have you been? We were beginning to worry about you." said Karen, concerned.

"Just trying to hurry the waiter to figure out what we owed so I could pay him."

"Gee, Rosie, I was going to treat tonight," Nancy said.

"No worries," I responded with a grin. "You can buy the nightcaps at Loews."

We happily regrouped on the patio at Loews after we retrieved Sweet Pea, yet my mind continued to wander, and I found it hard to concentrate on the girls' chatter and the tinkling of their laughter.

"Hey, girl, we're talkin' to you," Karen said with an Italian accent. She looked at me with a twinkle in her eye. "We've just been saying that it's good to see some of your 'ole' self again. You've kept us all worried ever since Jeff died, you know. You've been so distressed and saddened about what happened."

I felt my cheeks redden as I held up my thumb in victory. "It's about time to get some of the joy of living back, isn't it?" We fell silent, each with her own thoughts. I was tired and more than ready to go to bed. I wondered what tomorrow would bring and if, indeed, I would have what it would take to deal with things.

"Goodnight, all," said Nancy, the first to fold.

"Guess it's time for the rest of us to follow," remarked Susannah as she stood and scooped up her purse.

"Me too," added Karen. "I'm ready to hit the hay."

"Me as well," I said joining them.

As I was lying in bed, I reviewed my conversation with Brian. I sat straight up as I realized that he'd said they were searching for the big boss. There it was—B.B. big boss. (B.B. had been the initials on a love note attached to a large diamond ring Melissa's roommate and I'd found in her bureau). B.B. could be anyone. It didn't have to be a man, either; it could be a woman.

Could it be Big Bertha, also called Mama, my boss at the Purple Passion Lounge? She certainly was mean enough. What about the chief of police? The happenings of the past few days would certainly fall into line with his own actions at the time of Jeff's death. I snorted; death? "You mean murder, Rosie," I muttered.

What about Sophia's partner, Richard? He looked as tough as he sounded. What about Tony and Johnny, the two head bosses at the Purple Passion Lounge? Truth be told, I didn't have good feelings about any of them.

As I closed my eyes, I could feel excitement building within me. There was something to be said about being part of taking them all down, and I was glad to be involved.

CHAPTER 4

T he next morning, the clouds hung low, and the air was mild without harsh sunshine. I was on edge, waiting for something to happen. By the time I rolled out of bed, the girls were already on the outdoor balcony, whispering among themselves so they wouldn't wake me. Little were they aware that I'd been lying awake in bed for hours trying to rein in my worries.

Sweet Pea had long ago abdicated her position with me, going ahead to be with the girls. She now greeted me enthusiastically, complete with a wide smile. She brightened my mornings, and I was glad that she was along for this special little trip. I only hoped I could keep her safe—and the girls too, of course.

Susannah was the first to see me. "Hi, Sunshine. Guess what? We've the whole day to spend at the spa—massages, facials, and a 'mani-pedi' for each of us. What do you think?"

How perfect ... and safe. "I love it," I cried out, happy with the plan.

"I've already reserved the spa, so they can take all four of us at once. We just have to take turns, so two of us will have facials and their nails done while the other two get massages."

"Pretty neat, huh?" asked Karen as she handed me a fresh cup of coffee. I could feel tears spring to my eyes; I knew how fortunate I was to have these wonderful women in my life. I felt the worry lift from my shoulders as I sank down into one of the empty outdoor chairs and breathed a sigh of release.

I sensed a movement to my left, below the balcony, and glanced down to see a rather average-looking man with a navy Boston Red Sox cap walking along the path. Steve? It was a huge relief to know that he must be the protector Brian had mentioned would be here on the premises looking out for us. As we watched him make his way to the main part of the resort where the restaurants were located, the thought of food must have crossed all our minds, for Nancy and Karen both said in unison, "Let's eat."

We all laughed. "Anyone for a swim first?" I proposed.

"Why not?" Nancy responded.

We donned our bathing suits and made our way down the trail leading to the pool, with Sweet Pea following close behind. We squealed like little girls as we plunged into the cool water and paddled around. Afterward, as I was drying off, I turned around and saw a man staring at us. He was wearing a red Boston Red Sox hat, which threw me off. Hadn't he been wearing a blue one before? Was this even the same man?

When we began our walk back to our suite, we passed him. I called out, "Good morning."

He never responded. Instead, he turned away. He was wearing large, dark sunglasses and his hat low on his head, so I couldn't get a clear view of his face. It was strange that Sweet Pea never approached him to seek out an adoring pat as was customary for her with most people. I looked behind me to make sure that all the girls were following me. I didn't want us to get separated and have anyone left alone and vulnerable to ... who knew what?

Before leaving for the spa, I made sure Sweet Pea was securely locked in our suite and comfortable lying on my bed. Food and water were available for her in the kitchen area.

We were happy to enter the spa. As we did, the enticing mixed aroma of lavender and mint, which are used to freshen and relax, instantly surrounded us. We met the desk clerk and were shown lockers to hang the clothes we were wearing and were given white, fluffy robes we'd wear for the rest of our time there. While we waited in the separate lounge area that held herbal teas, special lemon water, and some healthy munchies, I sensed everyone was beginning to relax.

"This is the life, isn't it?" asked Susannah. We all nodded and smiled. Of all of us, Susannah would appreciate this day the most, for until we'd met at college, she'd never been in a spa before.

"Who wants to be the first two for the body massage, and who wants to do facials first?" asked Susannah.

"If it's okay with you all, I would like to go first for the body massage. I need to have my back muscles worked on before doing anything else," Nancy said.

"Sure thing," Susannah responded. "Why don't you join her, Rosie?"

"Sounds good to me." This would give me an opportunity to decide how I was going to identify which man—the one in the red Boston Red Sox baseball cap or the one in blue—was Steve.

As I lay there, stomach down on the table with my head in the facial support, I finally had enough quiet time to close my eyes and look back in my mind to picture the two men in their baseball caps. Their body shapes were definitely different. As I began to doze off, I knew what I was going to do.

After my massage, it was my turn to have a manicure, but first, I asked to use the telephone to make a call. I was sitting in the one-way front window and could see both men in their caps. They were in the lounging area outside the spa, sitting far apart, ignoring each other. Pretty soon I heard the resort intercom asking "Steve" to please report to the main desk area for a telephone call. After a minute or two, the first man I had seen, the one in the blue cap, casually got up from his chair. He nonchalantly walked toward the main building as if he were not the one called. At about the same time, the man in the red cap also got up and headed toward the main building, looking as if it might have been he who had been summoned.

I quickly hung up the phone and hoped that whoever came forward wouldn't discover I was the caller and calling from the spa. Meantime, before he got too far away, I leaned toward the window and took a hard look at the man in the red cap so that I'd be able to recognize him—even without the hat. He definitely was not eye-catching. He had a slightly heavier upper body than the other man, and his dark brown hair was barely visible underneath his cap. When he looked behind him, I saw he had a pink scar tracing his right jawline. I hated to think how he got that. My mind was racing. Who the hell was he? Who was the other man? Which one was our protector? Before I could get my answer, I was called back in for my nail appointment.

I found an opportunity to text Brian to ask him how to identify our protector. I also wanted to tell him what time we needed the limo to pick us up to go to The Smith Center for the performance of *Idaho*. He texted that Steve would drive us to The Smith Center and wait there to return us to Loews. There was nothing more about Steve's identification except that he was wearing a Boston Red Sox cap, and Brian didn't specify a red or a blue one. When I tried calling him back, there was no answer, so I left a voice mail saying simply "Call me."

By the end of our beauty treatments, we were eager to take a nap before we dressed for the night's big event. Strangely, I fell sound asleep in spite of my worries and didn't even stir to answer Brian's call when it came in. He'd left me a message, and thinking I had not understood his previous message, he said, "Rosie, just call him by his name and you'll know. Talk to you tomorrow." Men—why is it they find it so hard to communicate? Always a tug of war.

I'd gone overboard and bought an expensive black dress that was off the shoulders and fit me like my own skin. With the stretchy fabric and the way it was tucked in the front, it looked dynamite on me. It made me look sexy and slim. I had also purchased high-heeled shoes that we girls had names for because they were just so …

When I entered the room, the girls gasped and called out, "Oh my, Rosie, you look absolutely stunning."

In turn, I viewed them and returned the compliment. "And so do you all. Wow, we're going to have fun tonight, ladies."

My friends all wore elegant but slightly more classic dresses than I, and they also wore very stylish strappy heels. There was no doubt we'd make quite a foursome. We laughed at Sweet Pea when we saw her strut around the room as if she too were seeking a compliment. She soon tired of it and went to eat her dinner in the kitchen. We left her and walked to the exclusive restaurant next to the spa. Our dinner reservations were for 5:30, and although it was a bit early, we wanted to make sure we'd have enough time to enjoy a few cocktails before dinner and still make it to the 8 o'clock show.

We all exclaimed over the menu and settled on their special for dinner—sautéed scallops on a bed of angel hair pasta, with a classic lemon beurre blanc sauce. It was heavenly. We chose fresh fruit for dessert to cleanse our palates, and then we collected our things to head out to the limo. When we arrived at the main door of the resort, our limo was at the curb, with the back door wide open, waiting for us, and the driver was already in his seat. I was the last, but as I started to get in, my heart began to race as I felt something wasn't right. Karen grabbed my hand and pulled me in. Before I could even sit down, the car took off, and I landed hard in my seat.

"Whoa!" Nancy cried out. "What's going on?"

I leaned forward and asked, "Steve? Steve, is that you?"

The driver never looked around, but I saw the pink scar running down his jawline, and my heart began to pound. "Stop, stop this car right now."

"Sit down and relax, lady. We're not going to hurt you. We just want what's ours, capisce?"

"Of course I don't capisce. What is it with you guys that you won't understand I don't have whatever it is you want? Okay, enough, mister. Pull over now." I demanded as I rose and leaned toward him.

I looked back at the girls, who looked frightened by our speed down the road. I watched as Susannah calmly pulled her cell phone out and began dialing 911. As she waited for them to answer, she asked me, "What road are we on?"

"We just got onto Lake Mead Parkway, heading west just outside Lake Las Vegas."

"I wish you hadn't done that, girls." He pulled out a gun and held it up in the air. Susannah closed the phone and put it back into her bag before she'd completed her call.

"I've had enough, haven't you, Rosie?" called out Nancy.

"You bet. Right or left?"

"I'll do left; you go right," ordered Nancy.

Nancy crawled over the seat, put her arms around the driver's neck, and squeezed. At the same time, I knocked the gun from his hand and grabbed the steering wheel. Nancy was used to working with large animals, so she knew she could squeeze the carotid arteries in the neck to knock them completely out; apparently it was the same for humans. As the driver's foot slipped off the gas pedal and he went slack, the car began to gradually slow down. I turned the wheel, and when the limo finally came to a stop, we were quite a way down the road. We ended up in a large empty parking lot beside stores that had closed for the day. Breathless and in shock, we didn't move out of our positions for several long seconds, but then we all scrambled out of the car and stood there wondering what we were going to do with the man slumped unconscious in the driver's seat.

"I know exactly what we *should* do," said Karen, disgruntled. "We've come all this way to see the show tonight, and we're going. Let's just dump him here. Nobody'll know the difference. I'll drive."

"You can't do that," protested Susannah.

"Why not?" I asked.

"Yeah," said Nancy. "He'll be fine in an hour or so."

Susannah looked at all of us, then nodded her head in agreement. "C'mon, I'll help drag him out of the car."

We pushed and pulled him out, with Nancy once again applying pressure on his neck to make sure he wouldn't wake up right away.

Karen got into the limo's driver's seat, and I sat beside her. "Drive to the Green Valley Ranch Casino parking lot," I ordered. "I'll show you the way. We'll dump the limo there, and I'll call Uber to pick us up in the parking lot. Don't forget, everybody, we have to remember to put the limo's keys under the mat before we leave it there."

All of a sudden, it hit us what we had done, and we began to laugh hysterically. By the time we reached the casino, tears were rolling down our cheeks. The Uber driver was already there waiting for us. He looked at us and didn't say a word as we piled out of the limo and into his car. We had sporadic fits of laughter, and his looks of bewilderment made us start all over again. As we approached The Smith Center, we hurriedly reapplied our makeup before going in.

Idaho was a funny musical, exactly what we needed to see after what we'd been through. It was only during the break that I could respond to Brian's three text messages asking "Where are you? Are you all right?"

I decided to call him, and he sounded frantic. "What the hell is going on? Are you okay?"

"We're fine," I answered. "We ran into a little problem. The driver of the limo wasn't Steve, and he tried to kidnap us."

"So where did you stash the limo?" he asked with resignation.

"Is it your limo, or did it belong to the other guy?"

"Yes, it's ours. That's how I knew you were in trouble when I got the call from Steve."

"Is he okay?"

"Nothing a couple of aspirin and a good night's sleep won't cure. So where did you dump the limo, Rosie?"

"In the parking lot at the Green Valley Ranch Casino." After a pause, I asked, "Cowboy, are you sure it's safe for us to return to Loews?"

After hesitating, he answered, "Yes, I now have two men stationed there. Mike will now be there with Steve. Mike will be in the limo after the show to take you back to the resort. And Rosie? I'm not even going to ask what you did with the driver. I don't want to know."

"Are we in trouble?

"To be honest, I think anyone who tries to cross *you* is in trouble. Good night, and for God's sake, be careful, Rosie girl." There was a click, and he was gone.

CHAPTER 5

T omorrow was going to be our last full day together, so for tonight and onward, we made a
vow to stick together, no matter what. When our limo
rolled up to the curb to pick us up after the show, we
were huddled together in a pack and acted more like out-
of-control teenagers than grown women. We were laughing and poking each other, recalling some of the lines
from the show. I thought I saw Mike smile as we clambered into the limo.

After we settled in our seats, my friends eyed Mike,
giving him the once-over, and we looked at one another
and smiled. Nancy wiggled her eyebrows up and down
and tipped her head my way to indicate he might be a
"real catch" for me. I laughed out loud at her antics, and
the others joined in. Mike caught my eye in the rearview
mirror and smiled broadly.

My heart melted when I saw him do this, for I found him very attractive and was drawn to him in ways that competed with any feelings for Brian. When I'd worked at the lounge, he had acted as my boyfriend and lived in my house as my personal security guard under Brian's orders to protect me. I was pretty sure Sweet Pea had been missing him as much as I had. I hadn't mentioned Mike to my friends because I didn't want to worry them and have them think things were serious enough that I needed protection.

We met Steve when we got back to the resort as he held the door for us to get out. He seemed as nice as Mike, yet we all wondered why it was necessary to have two men protecting us. Protecting us from what?

In the morning, we gathered as usual for our cup of coffee before we began the day. With coffee in hand, Susannah called the four of us to a meeting. "Rosie, I couldn't sleep a wink last night worrying about you. In all good conscience, I can't fly out of here tomorrow. I'm not going to leave you here alone until I know you're safe."

"I feel the same way," said Karen.

"Me too," chimed in Nancy. "We have always worked well as a team to resolve whatever was happening in one of our lives when we needed each other. I think this is another thing we should do *together*."

I was floored, for I hadn't expected this at all, and I wasn't sure how I felt about it either. On the one hand, it would be great to have support from the best friends a girl could have. On the other hand, I didn't want any of them to get hurt.

I sat quietly and tried to collect my thoughts. I knew I could trust my friends—there was no doubt about that—but did it make any sense for them to get involved? What could they do? "Listen," I began, "I can't thank you enough for wanting to be there for me and to protect me from ... well, not even sure what. But I won't let you girls do that. You all have your own lives to live, and it just wouldn't be fair ..."

They all began talking at once, arguing their points. "Hold on," I interrupted. "I didn't say I couldn't use your help. I meant that there's another way around all this. Let me explain what I have in mind."

After I talked about different alternatives and explained—without divulging every little detail—what Brian, Mike, and I were trying to do, we raced to get dressed. We began making telephone calls to complete what we had in mind. My last call was to Mike, asking him to pull the limo to the front so we could run errands. I knew Brian wouldn't be happy to have us leave Loews, but there was no time to waste if we were to accomplish all we wanted to. Besides, he didn't get to vote on this. Even if he could, he would lose four to one.

Sure enough, word got back to him, and he called. I chose not to answer. Seconds later, he texted me. "Rosalie, you have to stop going off on your own. We're a team, remember? Please fill me in on what's happening. Call me."

In spite of myself, I grinned when I received his message, because he had used my full name, something my grandmother used to do when she was upset with me. I picked up my phone and dialed him.

"Rosie ..."

"Hey, Cowboy," I interrupted, "no worries. We're just going to run a few errands in town, and Mike will be with us. I promise we'll be back at the resort in time for cocktails on the terrace before dinner."

"I don't know what you're up to, but as a team, we have to be on the same page."

"I know," I agreed in a subdued manner. I knew that if we didn't work together, the whole investigation could go down the drain and no one would be held responsible for murdering Melissa and Sally. I definitely didn't want that to happen. I'd become even more determined to find the killer—or killers—of those beautiful girls. No one should get away with it simply because they were dancers on the Strip and "didn't count."

I heard Brian exhale a long sigh of resignation before adding, "Promise me that you girls will stick together, okay?"

"Okay. Wait, hold on just a minute—you've been holding back from *me* too. Two men to protect us? What exactly is going on?"

"We're not sure yet, which is why I have extra protection for you. Just keep safe, hear?"

"You take care too, Cowboy."

It felt weird, though good, to have Brian concerned about me, because it'd been a long time since any man worried about me at all. I realized that although I hadn't known Brian for very long, I felt as though I'd known him my entire life and could trust him. But could I?

After making hurried last-minute phone calls and Googling on our iPads to find the information we wanted, we headed out to meet Mike and the waiting limo. This time, we were dressed in casual cargo pants and cotton T-shirts. As we climbed in, each of us greeted Mike with a cheery hello and a smile. In turn, he seemed delighted to be "road running" with us.

The first stop was the Pleasure Me store—a store that featured sex toys—in the old downtown. When we told

Mike our destination, he blushed and asked, "What are you girls up to? Are you sure that's where you want to go, or are you teasing me?"

But that was exactly where we wanted to go. Karen had researched a nifty-looking lipstick—something most people wouldn't think of as dangerous that actually was pepper spray. It'd be handy to keep it in the pocket of our pants or have lying on our desks at work. I thought it was too bad I hadn't had it when I worked at the Purple Passion Lounge, for it was always best to have extra protection with you at all times, whether or not you needed it.

We went into the store together looking like a special ops team casing the joint. This wasn't the kind of place any of us was used to shopping in, and we gaped at everything there and even asked questions about how some of the items worked. Then we became entranced by the stylish and popular limited-edition large-face watches; however, these held a hidden recording device. We giggled and laughed over some of the other items and spent more time than we had anticipated. We walked out with bags full of lipstick pepper sprays, watches, and a few other items. When Mike saw us carrying our bags, he looked at each of us and just shook his head and tried to hide a smile.

"Okay, Mike. We're off to find a good place to eat lunch."

We ended up at the Cheesecake Factory, and of course, we invited Mike to join us. While we sat at a large table in the back of the restaurant, I was surprised by Mike's easy banter. He usually was quiet and very serious about being my protector, but this was something new, since I'd never seen him in a group before. He got us cracking up as he joked, "Why didn't the lifeguard save the hippie?" We looked at each other and shook our heads. "Because he was too far out, man." We laughed in spite of ourselves.

"That's so corny," Karen complained. "Haven't you got a better one than that? A newer one?"

Not to be shut down completely, Mike threw in, "You want to hear a pizza joke? Never mind, it's pretty cheesy." We groaned and pleaded for him to stop. "No more jokes, please."

Mike obviously was enjoying all the attention he was receiving from us and the people around us. They looked at us with curiosity, and then smiled when they saw we were simply having fun together.

"Okay, Mike," I said as we left the restaurant after we had filled our stomachs with pulled pork sandwiches. "Our last stop is the law library at UNLV. We'll be there for some time, so if you want to find something else to do, please feel free. We brought our laptops with us, so we can read or do something else while we're there. It's up to you."

"Oh, no, you don't," responded Mike. "I'm not letting you girls out of my sight for a minute. You know what Brian would say, right?" As we pulled into the school parking lot, he ordered, "You girls stay right here while I park the car."

I'd asked Susannah to research Nevada State law for precedents on withholding evidence in a murder case, even though it wasn't her expertise. She agreed even though she didn't know about Sophia's death and had few of the particulars of Melissa's or Sally's death. She said she trusted me, which was a huge relief, and she mentioned she wanted to look up some other things as well. She asked the rest of us to do some of the photocopying to save time.

It turned out to be a long afternoon, so we were glad to head back to Loews. When we got there, Sweet Pea was happy to see us and trailed close behind me. We donned our swimsuits for a last swim, because there'd be no time tomorrow for a dip—all the girls' return flights were among the first flights of the day out of McCarran International.

My cell phone rang, and it was Cindy, my friend from the Purple Passion Lounge who I'd worked with before the lounge closed. "Hi there, Rosebud," she said using the nickname she'd given me. "They want us back here at the lounge. They said we're the ones who know the front desk best, especially since Mama's no longer there. Have you heard they're telling everyone they are closed because they're doing 'a bit' of decorating and are going to reopen on Monday? Can you believe that?"

I just laughed—whatever. "Is Romano coming back too?" I asked. Romano was the chef at the lounge whom I'd befriended, and was my lifesaver by helping me to escape with the four little girls.

"He certainly is. Are you in?" she asked with anticipation in her voice.

It was good to hear Cindy's voice, and it didn't take me long to decide. "If you guys are going to be there, then I'm in. Otherwise, no."

"You're on, Rosebud. Don't forget, you and I have to meet with our head boss, Tony, before your shift, so come in around 2 o'clock, okay?"

I could hear her hesitation, but I thought I knew what she wanted to ask. "Mike's playing security guard for my friends and me. I'll tell him you called, all right?"

"Great, and tell that gorgeous man to call me. He's sure a tough one to tie down, isn't he?"

There was nothing I could say, for I thought it would indeed be hard for anyone to tie him down. I felt my heart twitch, because there was a part of me that would like to do just that. Cindy was hoping to have a relationship with him, and I wasn't sure whether that was going to work out for her. I didn't know how I felt about it either, but at the same time, I wanted to make sure that I didn't step on her toes, for she was becoming one of my dear friends. I didn't want to squelch that.

I got off the phone and turned back to my sister-friends. They were sitting in the living room reading or looking at their iPads while they waited for me to get off the phone. I saw Susannah glance at Nancy, who had a wide grin across her face. "I don't even have to say a word. I know what you're thinking," exclaimed Susannah.

"Margaritas at the pool, right?" Karen asked Nancy.

"You bet. Let's go."

Sweet Pea happily followed us there and stayed close beside me. We sipped our drinks, relieved to let go of our day and simply begin to relax. When I searched the area around us, I looked for anybody who looked out of place. Steve, our second protector, wandered down by the pool and pretended to ignore us. I didn't know where Mike was—probably napping.

There was only one family left in the pool, and they were already beginning to collect their things to leave. I felt myself relax even more, and when I looked at the other girls, I saw it in their faces too. We all were beginning to let go of our worries and ready to enjoy our time together.

Karen startled us with a full belly laugh. "Will you ever forget that wild ride we had with that jerk driver? Oh, my god, we must have looked like a car full of Muppets as we careened down the road."

We all began to roar with laughter and shout with glee, recalling every step that we'd taken to get to The Smith Center that night. Then we gathered in one large circle in the center of the pool, clasped arms, and hugged one another, vowing that no matter what, no one would be able to separate the four of us as best friends. We were friends for life, and how I loved them.

We chose to return to the same restaurant we had gone to that crazy night we attended the play *Idaho*, only this time, we would dine later and wouldn't have to leave early. We dressed more casually than before, though Susannah and Karen wore simple sundresses. The material of their dresses flowed around their bodies, making them look elegant and sophisticated. This was a new style for Karen, and she dazzled us with her fresh appreciation of herself.

Meanwhile, Nancy and I wore dressy black pants with matching designer tops, each in a style that suited us. We left Sweet Pea behind, napping once more on my bed.

As we walked the path toward the restaurant, we knew we were quite the beautiful foursome, each unique in her own way. With every step we took as a group, heads turned. We casually strolled toward our destination and simply nodded, smiled, or said hello to those watching us.

I had a feeling that something unpleasant was about to take place. I looked around and searched for the cause, but no one seemed out of place or threatening. I released a deep sigh of satisfaction and hoped it was all in my head.

The waiter placed us at a corner table apart from the main dining area in order to give us privacy. I took the corner seat with my back to the wall, which made it easy for me to scan the room inconspicuously. I always felt safer sitting that way because I could see anyone who approached and thus avoided being surprised.

After we ordered cocktails and began to discuss our day, I looked up to see Brian in the distance, searching the room, obviously looking for me. His face lit up when he saw me, and as he approached our table, I must have had an odd expression on my face, because Susannah asked, "Rosie, what's wrong? You look like you've seen a ghost."

At that, the girls turned around to watch Brian make his way toward us. He looked exceedingly handsome despite the frown that creased his forehead. I felt my face going from pale white to beet red as I waited for him, and my heart beat faster. The girls looked at me, then at him, and seemed to concur that he definitely was having an effect on me.

"Hi, Brian. What brings you here?" I inquired in the most professional voice I could muster.

"Hi, everyone," Brian said with a big smile on his face that belied the worry in his eyes. "Having a good time?"

"Everyone, this is Brian Boyce. Brian, meet Susannah, Nancy, and Karen." They all shook hands with Brian and gave him a huge smile. Susannah nodded toward me and said, "We've heard what you and Rosie have been up to. We hope you'll take good care of her and not let anything happen to her."

I watched Brian gain his composure, for it was obvious he wasn't used to the demands of being in charge of my safety. "I'm doing my best." He grinned at them, adding, "As I'm sure you already know, that's not always easy to do, what with Rosie's determination to go it alone ..." he trailed off. He forced a smile and asked, "Rosie, may I see you for a minute, please?"

As I paused, the girls watched to see my response. Brian was aware of my hesitation and said, "I promise it won't take long ... just a minute or two."

I got up from my seat and turned to the others. "I'll be right back." For some reason, I was annoyed with Brian for having interrupted us. Was it so important he couldn't just text or call me, or was this his way of meeting my friends?

Why did he have to come here and draw attention not only to himself but also to me, who was left to trail along behind him?

I followed him to the outside veranda next to the restaurant, which, fortunately, was empty and quiet. "What's up, Cowboy?" I asked, with an edge to my voice.

"My friend in the news department called me late this afternoon to give me a heads-up on a potential story. I wanted to warn you in person about what you might be facing. Your name was leaked to the press as the one who 'kidnapped' the girls, and the chief of police is making noises about having you arrested for endangering minors."

"You've got to be kidding," I burst out in exasperation.

"I wish I were. Let's plan to meet tomorrow to discuss the situation and how we should proceed. In the meantime, if anyone should recognize and approach you, asking questions, just respond, 'No comment.'"

My heart fell and my eyes watered as I nodded my head in affirmation. "Are the girls okay? Where are they now?"

"They're in one of the safe houses, and they're protected—the people who work to prevent human trafficking are taking over. They'll be fine," he added soothingly.

He shoved a newspaper toward me, and I saw that my picture had been taken after I returned to the Purple Passion Lounge following my escape with the girls. I didn't even remember its being taken. "My god," I remarked impulsively, "look at my hair."

There it was in print. My hair made it difficult not to draw attention. I could see Brian trying to bite back a smile.

My stomach began to roil at the thought of what might lay ahead, and I pushed the newspaper back into his hand. As I did so, he reached out to pull me toward him, but I turned and stepped away so he couldn't touch me. I was too vulnerable. I couldn't stand the idea of falling apart right now, especially with the girls waiting for me to return.

"Rosie?" he asked.

I shook my head no. I headed back into the restaurant, stifling my anguish and any tears. That was no way to end the last night with my best friends. When I opened the door to enter the restaurant, I turned back to see Brian standing there, looking lost.

"What was that all about?" asked Karen as I approached the table.

"Nothing, really. He wanted to make sure I was able to meet with him tomorrow, that's all."

Even though they suspected it might be more than that, once they saw the unyielding expression on my face, the girls knew better than to ask more questions. Speaking for the group, Nancy piped up, "Rosie, don't give up. The fat lady hasn't sung yet."

"I'll let you know when I hear the first note, I promise you," I answered with a slight smile. "I'll fill you in each week when we have our group call." That was something we had agreed upon that morning. Every week, or sooner if necessary, I'd call or text them as a group to fill them in on what was happening on my end. Or if need be, I'd make a separate telephone call to Susannah, who'd reach Karen and Nancy to fill them in. We sat in silence for a few minutes, digesting what had been said. "Right now, ladies, I think it's time for a fresh round of drinks on me. What do you say?" I asked.

"Perfect timing," Nancy said to the waitress, who was serving several appetizers, which they must have ordered while I was outside with Brian. We all smiled at Nancy as, with a pleased expression, she filled her plate and sniffed what she had put on it—several grilled cocktail shrimp, served with a mustard-aioli sauce, and some Parma ham wrapped around grilled asparagus and thin slices of melon.

"It's just not fair," complained Karen. "You get to eat all you want and don't even gain an ounce."

"What can I say? Just lucky, I guess. Besides, what are you talking about? You're in the best shape ever."

"My dear, sweet Nancy, it's because I don't eat everything I want to," responded Karen.

"Well then, it's working," Nancy said with a mischievous grin.

Susannah and I looked at each other and chuckled. This back and forth between Nancy and Karen had been going on for years, and it was something we all laughed about each time we got together. Karen winked at me and smiled.

We each had the special entrée, a pasta dish with chicken and asparagus in a light lemon wine sauce, topped with toasted almond slivers, tasty and not too heavy. Then we ordered lemon mousse cake to share, which turned out to be delightful. I sneaked a peek at Nancy, who was seriously struggling to finish her part of the dessert. I winked at Susannah and Karen, who were watching her too. Nancy had eaten most of the appetizers, which must have filled her up.

"I know, I know, this is unusual—my not finishing everything. But boy, oh boy, it sure was fun trying." She grinned at all of us.

"It's time for a glass of Amaretto and sparkling water to settle our stomachs," I announced as I called the waitress to our table.

We became quiet as we finished our nightcaps, and then we slowly walked back to our suite and hugged each other as we went. It was going to be hard for us to part, as it always was after we spent any time together. Before ending the night, we hugged again as a group, kissed each other, and said how much we loved one another. Then we separated to complete packing before going to bed. As I picked up the tarot cards lying on the coffee table, they fell out of my hands, so I knelt to pick them up. Most had stayed together, and it was easy to quickly gather them in one swoop and push them together. One fell out. As I reached for it, I saw it was the Death card. I put it back into the deck with certainty that someone else was going to show up dead; I could feel it in my bones. I wondered who it would be this time.

CHAPTER 6

W hy is it when you didn't want morning to come, it arrived with a cacophony of sounds — alarms ringing, showers running, coffee grinding, whispers that sounded like shouts, and, in my case, Sweet Pea on my stomach making happy sounds while trying to reach my face with wet kisses? I looked at the clock to see it was just 4 a.m., time to get up, get dressed, and arrive at the airport in plenty of time for the girls to check in for their early-morning flights. I jumped out of bed and called Mike to remind him we'd be ready to be picked up at 5 o'clock as agreed.

"Hey, Sunshine." called Karen, who was already dressed and leaning against the doorframe of the bedroom. "You sure were sleeping like the dead. You never even moved when I got up."

51

"Oh, please, don't even mention the word dead," I said with a laugh, feeling my heart skip a beat.

"I'm worried about you, Rosie. Are you really going to be all right if we leave?" she asked in a worried tone.

"Absolutely. Brian, Mike, and Steve have my back."

"I'm going to be happy to have all of this end so I know you're safe. You can back out, you know. There's always my place for you and Sweet Pea to escape to like you did before."

Remembering the time I had done just that after Jeff's death and knowing I always had a safe haven with Karen—or Susannah or Nancy, for that matter—made me feel warm all over. I was fortunate to have them in my life.

As we piled into the limo, Mike's smile was not as bright as usual, and I knew he'd also miss the girls. There was none of the usual laughter and banter between us, for we became lost in our own thoughts. The silence became deafening until Mike couldn't stand it anymore and started to sing a little ditty.

"There once was an old lady who swallowed a fly,
I don't know why she swallowed a fly—perhaps she'll die.
There was an old lady who swallowed a spider
That wriggled and wiggled and tiggled inside her.
She swallowed the spider to catch the fly,
I don't know why she swallowed a fly—perhaps she'll die."

We all looked at each other and laughed. I don't know why Mike had chosen this particular song, but it was perfect for us because we used to sing it together while horsing around at Cornell. We joined in, much to Mike's pleasure, and it must've been a sight for any bystanders to hear us through the open windows of the limo as we sang loudly and intermittently punctuated the performance with laughter.

> There was an old lady who swallowed a bird,
> How absurd to swallow a bird.
> She swallowed the bird to catch the spider,
> She swallowed the spider to catch the fly,
> I don't know why she swallowed a fly—perhaps
> she'll die.

> There was an old lady who swallowed a cat,
> Fancy that, to swallow a cat.
> She swallowed the cat to catch the bird,
> She swallowed the bird to catch the spider,
> She swallowed the spider to catch the fly;
> I don't know why she swallowed a fly— perhaps
> she'll die.

We giggled and laughed until tears rolled down our cheeks. Mike kept thumping the steering wheel in time with the music while singing at the top of his lungs.

> There was an old lady that swallowed a dog,
> What a hog, to swallow a dog.
> She swallowed the dog to catch the cat,
> She swallowed the cat to catch the bird,
> She swallowed the bird to catch the spider,
> She swallowed the spider to catch the fly.
> I don't know why she swallowed a fly—perhaps
> she'll die.

Mike's voice began to fade as we reached the end of the song.

> There was an old lady who swallowed a cow,
> I don't know how she swallowed a cow.
> She swallowed the cow to catch the dog,
> She swallowed the dog to catch the cat,
> She swallowed the cat to catch the bird,
> She swallowed the bird to catch the spider,
> She swallowed the spider to catch the fly.
> I don't know why she swallowed a fly—perhaps she'll die.
> There was an old lady who swallowed a horse.
> She's dead, of course.

The last words of the song sobered us all. It was time to say goodbye. There was not a dry eye among us, including Mike's, though he pretended he had something in his.

We all clambered out of the car, hugged, and kissed, and then Mike and I watched them walk away. He put his arm around me, held me close, and whispered, "Everything's going to be okay. You'll see. I'll protect you."

Instead of dropping the limo off as he had intended, Mike insisted on keeping me in his sight. He'd take me back to the resort so that I could pick up Sweet Pea and my car to drive home. Although Steve was scheduled to do that, Mike called Brian to say he would.

Secretly, I felt relieved that Mike again would be staying with me for the next few days as my protector—and supposed boyfriend. It had been nice the last time he had been in the house with Sweet Pea and me. I had forgotten how comforting it could be to share small talk and meals with someone you enjoyed, and I was looking forward to doing that again.

"Mike, I'll need some time to repack my things and walk Sweet Pea. Is that all right? I thought we'd also grab something to eat here at the resort before we leave, because as it is, we'll need to get in some groceries for home."

"Sure. I have to pack up my things as well, and I need to check in with Brian to see what he wants us to do."

"Did I tell you I'm going back to work at the Purple Passion Lounge?"

His surprised expression made me realize I hadn't said anything to Brian either. "When?" he asked.

"Tomorrow."

"It's a mess there. I don't know if Brian will want you to do that."

I could feel my face burn as I held back my frustration. "Sorry, but you and Brian don't get to vote on this. I've already promised Cindy and Romano I'd be there, and I don't intend to leave them stranded."

I watched Mike for his reaction upon hearing Cindy's name. She certainly was interested in him, but was he interested in her? His expression remained neutral.

We drove into Loews, and Mike dropped me off at the front entrance. I felt something was wrong, so I hurried to my room. As I rushed down the hall and approached my suite, I thought I saw movement at the end of the hallway, and as I got closer, I saw the door to the suite was ajar. My heart stopped. What was going on? I raced into the front room with my heart beating. It was quiet—no sound anywhere. Where was Sweet Pea?

My heart fell. My dog meant everything to me, and I would be lost without her. I hoped nothing had happened to her, but where was she? I rushed to my bedroom and saw my clothes scattered all over the floor and the chest drawers open. Since I was the last one up this morning and knew I'd be returning, I hadn't made the bed. The covers were thrown back and bunched at the bottom. As I looked more closely, I saw Sweet Pea, just her black nose and one eye peeking out. When she realized it was me, she bounded out of the covers and leapt into my arms. I hugged her close and covered her sweet face with many kisses.

I hated it when people accused dogs of not being smart or unable to remember things after just a short time. I knew that wasn't true for Sweet Pea, as she had a sixth sense that amazed me. Perhaps it was Gram who helped protect her, but no matter, I knew that whoever had been in the suite hadn't realized Sweet Pea was there. She must have sensed trouble and remained hidden and quiet.

It didn't take me long to clean up the clothes strewn around and pack them and my essentials. "C'mon girl, let's take a nice long walk around the lake. Does that sound good to you?"

She bounced at my feet. I reached for her leash and hooked her up, and we headed out. The day was glorious, with a slight breeze and a cloudless azure sky. We went to the front patio area, where I expected Mike to be waiting for us, but he was nowhere to be seen. I looked at Sweet Pea, and she gave me an intense look in return. I got her message—she needed to be walked *now*. We navigated the different levels of the patio until we hit the pathway.

I felt a heavy sense of doom and tried to shake it off. The day was too beautiful for sadness. I loved my friends, and as sorry as I was to see them go, I was relieved not to have them with me because I was afraid they'd get hurt, and I didn't want that to happen. I was ruminating over this as we walked the path when I heard Sweet Pea growl.

When I looked up, I saw approaching us the same man who had followed me on the trail before. He raced toward us but looked distracted and didn't seem to be paying attention to what lay ahead of him. I held my breath as he got closer and closer. I stepped entirely off the path to avoid him, and he ran right past me. Only Sweet Pea's barking at the last drew his attention, and I knew he'd seen and recognized me, but he never stopped running and continued on.

This is crazy, I thought. What is he running from? I hurried down the trail past a section heavily lined with bushes on either side, and we entered a space that opened up onto a larger view of the lake. The water, rippling with barely a sound, was murky, as usual. I saw what looked like a log floating about 10 feet away. As I began to study it, I could more easily make out its odd shape, and I realized it wasn't a log at all. As one of the small waves nudged it, I saw what looked like a hand that rose up from the water and floated on top. A body? Someone dead? Another murder?

I pulled out my phone to call Mike and was surprised to hear him call out from the trail behind us, "Rosie? Sweet Pea?"

"Mike. Over here."

"I thought you were going to meet me on the patio." he barked, irritated.

"Sorry. You weren't there, and Sweet Pea couldn't wait," I apologized. "Look, Mike, look out there in the water. It looks like a body, doesn't it?"

"Oh, my god, it sure does."

I watched Mike look around, searching the area, and he turned to me. "Help me, Rosie. Haul that branch over there to me. I'll see if I can use it to drag the body closer to shore."

While I was doing that, Mike put in a quick call to Brian. After I dragged the long, heavy branch to Mike, he hoisted it with some difficulty, hefted it across the water, and lowered it onto the body. After a few tries, a limb on the branch snagged on the clothing, and he began to slowly pull the body in toward us.

He was trying not to let the branch touch any of the exposed skin, as he knew it was important not to destroy any evidence. Nevertheless, the twig snapped, and the branch caught on the outside of the body. Mike tried to unhook it, grunting loudly, and then, with a sudden yank, he flipped the body over and snapped, "Damn it. Now look what I've done."

As he tugged the body nearer the shore, we stood looking at it, not saying a word. David Masterly from the Purple Passion Lounge was staring sightlessly back at us.

In some ways, I felt sorry it was David, even though he had to have known what was going on at the lounge with the drugs and human trafficking. But why had someone killed him? It seemed odd that he had been murdered, for he seemed harmless in comparison with others at the lounge who had more authority and power. The tangled web of crime connected to the lounge was getting more and more sticky. It was going to be interesting to see who was left standing.

Sweat was pouring down Mike's face from all his efforts in the past 20 minutes or so. He wiped his face with his sleeve and looked at me in disbelief. "Do you believe this? What's going on?"

"I don't know what to say. Why was he even here?" I asked—but didn't receive a response.

Brian must not have been too far from Loews when he got the call from Mike, because as we stood there, we heard him coming down the trail. I picked up Sweet Pea so she wouldn't interfere with Brian and she wouldn't be able to sniff the body. After wiggling around and trying to escape from me to run and greet Brian, Sweet Pea finally settled down in my arms.

"Hey there," he greeted us solemnly. "Let's see what we've got here." He walked to the edge of the lake and studied what Mike had dragged to the shoreline.

Brian looked back at me, shaking his head. He said, "Rosie girl, you are like a magnet for corpses, aren't you?"

I simply nodded my head. He added, "I've called for the coroner and the others and asked them to arrive without making any disturbance, if at all possible. I don't want this to get out to the press right away. We've got too many loose ends to clean up first."

"Remember the man I told you about the other day, the one I think broke into my house? I saw him running from this direction as Sweet Pea and I were headed this way. He was in a hurry. At first, I thought he was coming for me, but he never stopped and ran right past us. I think he recognized me, though. Could he have something to do with this?"

"Maybe. Do you remember what he was wearing?"

I closed my eyes and described what I saw. "He was wearing black jeans and a white T-shirt with sleeves rolled up like in the '60s. He was about your height, had dark brown hair, and was wearing aviator sunglasses and a black baseball cap."

Immediately, Brian pulled out his phone to make a call and said, "Check every corner of this property, and see if you can find him without causing a scene. When you have him in custody, call me right away."

After Brian ended the call, Mike asked, "What do you want us to do now?"

"Let's get Rosie out of here. I don't want her connected to this in any way, especially after she was mentioned in the newspaper, connected to the lounge. Go back to her house and get her settled in. Let's meet later. I'll call you."

"Why don't you plan to eat with us tonight? I'll fix dinner," I said.

Brian regarded me. "A home-cooked meal is the best offer I've had in a long time. Count me in."

"Okay," I agreed. "That's the plan, Stan." I said, glad he'd be joining us that evening.

CHAPTER 7

A fter we got home, I unpacked, started a load of laundry, and called to Mike, "Ready to go?"

He closed his iPad and got up. "As ready as I'll ever be."

We said goodbye to Sweet Pea, who could hardly keep her eyes open after all the upset she'd been through that day. This was one time she was glad to be left home.

"Same store, Rosie?"

Once again, Mike and I selected items for dinner and some other upcoming meals. I didn't know what it was about shopping for groceries, but it went one of two ways for me—either I was sick of food altogether, or everything looked good. Mike watched me pile an abundance of food into my basket but didn't say a word. He continued to watch me as I carefully picked through the fruit.

"Is there any piece of fruit you haven't touched yet?" he teased.

"I know," I laughed, "I like to make sure I've picked the best one."

"I didn't realize you were so fussy," he remarked.

"About everything," I answered with a wide smile.

I ended up choosing ingredients for a chicken casserole recipe that was easy to make and not too rich. I'd serve it with sweet black rice, something new for me. A salad and a choice of wines would complete the meal. I didn't know whether either Brian or Mike would have a glass of wine with dinner, but I wanted to make sure there was plenty to choose from if they decided to join me.

I still hadn't said anything to Brian about my returning to the lounge, and I didn't know what his response would be. However, I felt it was imperative we soon finish what we had started to uncover the culprit or culprits in Melissa's and Sally's deaths, or it would become something the police would push aside as they worked on more recent cases.

I was looking forward to working with Cindy again, for I felt we had bonded, perhaps because of all we'd endured together working at the Purple Passion Lounge. I admired her for having followed her own strong convictions without regard for the consequences of her actions by coming to my aid to ensure the safety of the little girls. I was pleased we were becoming friends.

And my darling chef, Romano, from the lounge. He was such a lifesaver at that time. How could I ever thank him enough for all he'd done to help me protect the girls from their nasty fate? He was a man dear to my heart, and that made my return to the lounge even sweeter. I was such a lucky lady to be able to call him my friend for many reasons, not the least of which was his spoiling me with his cooking. I chuckled to myself as I wondered what he had in mind for my next delectable treat.

The doorbell rang, and Sweet Pea went nuts when she saw it was Brian. This time, he reached down to pick up her wiggling body and held her close. I could see he was tired and needed some comfort in addition to all the happy licks he was receiving from Sweet Pea. "Hi there, Cowboy." I greeted him, heartily.

"Hey, Rosie. Where's Mike?"

"In the living room. Did you find the guy I was talking about?" I asked as I followed him to where Mike was sitting.

"Not yet, and I don't know if we will. I'll need you to describe him to our artist so he can create a likeness, and we can run him through our files to see if we can identify him. Chances are he has a record. We'll call the artist in the morning to set up a time, okay?"

Knowing what Brian's reaction might be when I told him about my returning to the lounge, Mike excused himself. "I'm just going to take Sweet Pea for a quick walk. C'mon, girl."

Sweet Pea perked up at "walk," but I could tell she had no desire to leave Brian's side. It was going to be interesting to see how Mike handled the situation. Without hesitating, he strode to the couch, scooped up Sweet Pea, and left with a very surprised dog in his grasp. I had to smile.

"Cowboy, there's something you should know. I'm going back to work at the lounge tomorrow when it reopens. They've called both Cindy and me in. They said they needed us to run the front desk since Mama's no longer there."

Brian's face got all red. I watched him consider how to react. Finally he let out a long sigh. "I guess there's nothing I can do to stop you, is there? I just want to make sure you're safe, that's all. Maybe with both Mama and David Masterly no longer around, things will be better there, but let's work *together* to come up with an action plan. How about meeting tomorrow?"

"Sure." I could see Brian was exhausted and in no shape to concentrate on anything tonight. The poor guy needed a break, as did Mike.

Mike returned a few minutes later, and I completed the salad. Not much later, the casserole was cooked and ready to serve. As we sat at the table, I asked them, "Would you like a glass of wine?"

They looked at each other and said in unison, "Yes, please."

Any tension in the air due to the events of the previous few days began to dissipate, for which we all were grateful. I had already enjoyed some of Mike's silly humor, but it was Brian's humor that brought me unexpected pleasure. His laughter was full and deep as he told "war stories" of the two of them in the field together. "Do you remember when we had to dress in drag, Mike? Or remember ..."

The evening ended with the three of us sitting and relaxing in the living room. Before I knew it, both Mike and Brian were slumped over on the couch, snoring. I tapped Mike on the shoulder, and he jerked awake. I put my finger across my lips and motioned for him to get up. Together we lifted Brian's legs onto the couch, and I draped a blanket over him. We left him to dream his dreams, and we both headed upstairs to bed, each to our own room.

As I slipped on my nightclothes, I thought about all that had happened in the previous few weeks. There were still so many loose ends to clean up. Without knowing all the connections, it seemed almost impossible that we'd be able to resolve anything quickly. We still had to find out who had killed Melissa, Sally, and Sam and determine whether their deaths were connected. Who was going to apprehend those responsible for trying to sell the girls? What about those who wanted to purchase them? What about the drugs? Did all of this fit together? It all was a mess.

I thought of David Masterly floating in the lake and sensed that he probably wouldn't have been all that unhappy about dying, as he was already dead in his own heart, and he looked it as well. I don't believe I've ever seen a person so sad, emaciated, and lacking zest for life. I was pretty sure that he'd been in love with Melissa, and it seemed likely he was the one who gave her the diamond ring with the love note signed by B.B. If Melissa really wanted to turn her life around, David would have been a great choice to help her do that—even if he were double her age. But what was he doing out at Loews? How did his wife fit into it all? Lord, Mama was so unpleasant yet wielded power. Why?

The best way for me to get answers was to let my mind flow so I was freely open to visions and thoughts, and I'd be able to view events and, I hoped, make some sense of it all. I closed my eyes and once again saw the faces of the four little girls whom I had helped escape the traffickers.

As my mind wandered, I knew I'd soon have to write an article for my new column in *Women Living Well*. Maybe it should be about human trafficking. There is so much more of that going on than I ever imagined—all for sex— and it made me sick to think about it. I thought about the little girls and wondered where they'd come from. All four of them spoke Spanish—only one spoke a bit of English as well. I'd see whether I could interview her.

It would be interesting to see who was in charge at the lounge tomorrow. Was Tony still in control? I yawned and stretched. Before I knew it, I had slipped into my own nightmare of worries. Once again, I was being chased by someone I didn't recognize. My feet were so heavy I could move only in slow motion and knew I was going to be taken down. I jerked awake, filled with dread. I was almost afraid to close my eyes again but did so in spite of myself. Tomorrow was on its way, and I needed to be rested and ready for all it held.

CHAPTER 8

I t was the smell of coffee brewing that woke me, so I knew Mike must be in the kitchen, doing his usual thing. I threw on my cashmere robe and headed downstairs only to find Brian sitting on the couch, holding his head. For a moment, I'd forgotten he'd spent the night. He didn't look very awake, and he kept gently pushing Sweet Pea away as she tried to lick his face. Obviously, he wasn't in the mood to play.

"Good morning, Sunshine," he greeted me hoarsely.

"Good morning to you. Gosh, you look like you've had a fight with yourself all night long." I said with a chuckle as I eyed his disheveled state.

"That's about the truth of it," he replied with a grin, dragging his fingers through his hair as if to comb it.

"Morning, Mike." I called out as I entered the kitchen, with Brian not far behind me.

"Oh, man, that coffee sure smells good," Brian exclaimed. "Not at all like at the TV station," he added.

Mike nodded toward the table. "Just sit down, you two, and I'll fix the eggs just the way you like them, Rosie."

"Hmmm, this is the life," I sighed with pleasure. "I love to be waited on."

Brian raised an eyebrow but said nothing. "I know," I said, as I looked at him. "Don't get too used to this; we've got work to do, right?"

Brian gave a quick nod. "Mike, we need to find out whether or not we're still welcome at the Purple Passion Lounge. Guess we should stick to the plan of your driving Rosie into work as usual and play it like that."

"Right on, boss," replied Mike, giving me a wink.

It was almost overwhelming for me to see these two men in my kitchen. Both were strikingly handsome, each in his own way, and quite a catch for some lucky girl. It would be interesting to see what, if anything, came of our relationships, I thought.

"Rosie, when you're at the lounge, make note of all the changes there. Snoop around to see if you can find out anything about David Masterly's murder, okay? See what Cindy knows too."

As soon as Brian mentioned Cindy's name, I saw him glance at Mike to check for any reaction, but again there was nothing. Guess Brian was as curious as I was about that.

I dressed more casually than I had for the days I had worked at the Purple Passion Lounge. I wore loosely tailored dark brown pants and a top to match, though I didn't think it would really matter what I wore. I put the spray lipstick the girls and I had bought in the pocket of my pants. It fit perfectly, and I was glad to have that extra protection, just in case. You never know …

I went downstairs to my office and rearranged the tarot cards on my desk. I held my breath, but nothing dropped out, thank God. We didn't need any more bodies showing up; we already had enough to deal with. The last Death card I had seen had been at Loews, and it obviously indicated David Masterly's death.

Since Cindy had asked me to come in early for our meeting with Tony, I called out to Mike, "Are you ready yet?"

Mike was serious as we drove and didn't say much. When we got to the front door of the lounge, he came around to open my door and stood by me for several seconds. Then he grabbed me tight and whispered, "Rosie, I want you to be very careful today. I don't want anything to happen to you, understand?"

I nodded, and before I could respond, he gave me an enthusiastic kiss on the lips. Oh my.

I ducked inside without saying a word, and through the one-way window, I watched him drive away. I could feel my face burn as I realized Cindy must have seen us. I didn't want to upset her, but there was no one at the desk.

I looked around and noticed a lot of new tropical plants. Someone was obviously trying to give this front area a more friendly appearance to make it look less like a corporation, and I liked it. Cindy came around the corner, and my heart leapt, for she was a sight for sore eyes. We hugged each other before she grasped me by the shoulder and said, "C'mon, the meeting's about to start."

We raced down the hallway, and I stopped at the entrance to the kitchen. Romano was standing in the middle of his kitchen directing a red-faced, frustrated worker who was holding a paintbrush, "No, there, in the corner, you missed a spot in the corner," Romano pointed out.

When Romano saw me, he came over, and we air-kissed several times before he exclaimed, "Oh, my darling Rosebud, I'm so glad to see you. There's so much going on here—it's such a mess. I'll have to catch you up. Come see me later, all right?"

Cindy watched us with a smile. She pulled on my sleeve, and we were off. "C'mon, hurry."

"Where are we going?"

"Down to the pool area for our meeting."

I could smell the chlorine as we got closer, which reminded me of what had been planned for that space—the sale or auction of four young girls by a human trafficking ring. It made me feel ill. As we entered, I could see the manager, Tony Angelo, sitting at one of the larger café tables. Sitting next to him was Johnny, facing us. Was he there as part of the management team or as protection for Tony?

There was an older woman sitting across from Tony whom I had seen once before during my previous days at the lounge. I thought she was the accountant, but I wasn't exactly sure what her role was.

As we moved forward to join them, Tony said, "Now that we're all here, let's get started. Cindy, Rosalie, thank you for coming. We have a lot to discuss, so let's get going."

As we sat down, I sensed tension emanating from the three already seated. "First of all, Rosalie, I want to thank you for protecting those four young girls. We had no idea Mama had put that in place. That's the last thing we want the Purple Passion Lounge to be known for, right?"

Memories of what had happened to my fiancé came flooding back. I got it—as others had done to Jeff, they were setting Mama up to take the fall for everything. I almost felt sorry for her. I also realized Cindy and I were in deep trouble, because as soon as Tony had spoken the words "thank you," I knew he was lying. He was furious with both of us but needed us to play the game so that he'd be let off the hook. The problem was that I hated playing games, and I was pretty sure Cindy did too.

When we didn't respond, he continued, "This past month has been difficult, to say the least, with all the deaths, the escapade with the young girls, and, of course, the drugs. It's imperative we stick together as a family to clear up this mess. You do understand, both of you, you are now part of the family?"

My heart fell because I knew exactly what he meant—the family was the Family (Mafia), and there usually was no way out. I wasn't willing to be a part of that but had no choice but to play along at this time. I felt Cindy flinch at his remark, but neither of us responded.

Tony continued, "You two will be in charge of signing our guests in, collecting the slips from the girls, and calling for PUP. We're still using them as our taxi service. I don't want anyone but you two and your reliefs to work the front desk until my cousin comes from back East to take over Mama's position. Understand?"

Although I already knew the answer, I asked, "Is Mama ever going to come back?"

Tony didn't answer right away, but then he said firmly, "Mama won't ever work here again. She's out on bail until her trial begins. If anyone asks either one of you anything about her, you're not to give out any information—about her or anything else. Capisce? If I find out that you have, there *will* be consequences. You can count on it."

As we sat in silence, he announced, "Rosalie, you'll have no more trouble from the chief of police. That's a dead issue."

I got goose bumps all over my body just hearing the word "dead." Tony squirmed in his chair and then leaned forward, adding, "By the way, David Masterly is no longer working here either. You'll report to Johnny from now on."

Cindy and I looked at each other, then nodded in agreement. Tony asked, "Sylvia, is there anything you'd like to add?"

Sylvia, the accountant, shifted in her chair, made uncomfortable by having the focus on her. "Just make sure the slips the girls hand you are clearly marked so there is no confusion about what they had going on." She paused for a fraction of a second and added, "I think you've covered everything else, Tony."

"Well, then, that's it," stated Tony, but he remained seated and waved his hand at us as though pushing us away. He stayed with Johnny and watched us as we left.

I felt his eyes drilling into us, which made me very uncomfortable. As soon as we got outside the pool room, Cindy and I clutched each other, and I whispered, "Man, we are in so much trouble."

"We sure are," confirmed Cindy.

I'd have to inform Brian and Mike about our situation as soon as I could, for it was looking as though we'd have to include Cindy in our investigation. That would make things interesting for sure, I thought with some trepidation.

Cindy waited for me to finish my thoughts before we moved forward, holding hands like best friends walking to grade school. When we reached the kitchen, we both automatically turned in, searching for Romano. When he saw us, he came forward and air-kissed the two of us saying, "My beautiful little flowers ..."

We looked around the kitchen and smiled. Romano was having the room painted a pleasant coral color. "Do you like?" he asked, spreading his arms and gesturing around the room.

"It's really beautiful," I responded, meaning it. "I wouldn't have picked this color, but it's perfect for here, it really is. It's cozy, sophisticated, and just the right touch."

"Yes, perfect," agreed Cindy, with a smile.

We tried not to be obvious as we looked around the kitchen hoping for one of Romano's treats. He didn't disappoint, as he called out, "Follow me. I've got something I want you two to try."

Cindy and I looked at each other with wide grins and tagged along behind him. He went to the stove and stirred a large pot of fresh soup. I began to salivate as I breathed in the aroma. He handed us each a spoon, and we dipped it into the pot. "Want a big bowl?" he asked.

Romano was a genius as far as I was concerned, for everything he created was 'beyond the beyond.' He served us, then pulled up another stool and sat beside us at the prep table. "While you girls were gone, I came into work every day to get my kitchen back in order. If only you could've seen the mess the FBI made with fingerprinting powder and dumping out every item in the storage area. What pigs. It took me hours and hours to get it all back together again."

Both of us made soothing sounds, shaking our heads at what he'd had to endure. Then I asked though a mouthful of soup, "So what else happened while we were gone?"

"Yeah," added Cindy, "spill."

Romano leaned in closer. "Mama was furious that you had taken the girls, my little Rosebud. She told the chief of police that you needed to be arrested for kidnapping them. He told her, 'Shut up and keep quiet because whatever you say can be held against you,' even though he hadn't officially read her the Miranda rights. She vowed to get even with you, so just be warned," he ended, looking deep into my eyes as I registered worry in his.

I felt a moment of panic. He added, "I guess they haven't figured out yet who helped you, because I heard Johnny warn Tony not to even try—to let everything else go. If he didn't, things could get worse."

"So what're we going to do?" I asked. "We'll have to be extremely careful now."

Cindy was the first to respond. "We're going to do whatever they need us to do until we can figure things out. Right, Rosebud?"

"Agreed. How about you, Romano?"

"Count me in," he answered in a lower tone of voice, filled with bravado.

"What else did you hear, Romano?" I asked with curiosity.

"Well," he whispered, puffing himself up, "I overhead Tony and Johnny arguing. Tony said that nobody was going to take *him* down. Then Johnny said, 'Let's close down for the next few days. We'll tell everyone we're closed for renovations and see if the FBI will let us reopen on Monday.'"

"So that's who came up with that idea," I said. I wondered what Johnny's real role was here, as it sounded as though it was more than security for the front area. I wondered why they really wanted me back. I could understand their wanting Cindy back because she'd been here for the previous nine months and had taken over some of David Masterly's responsibilities, but why me?

As I sat there with Romano and Cindy, the answer came. I realized that of course they wanted me back playing the role of the heroine representing Tony and the management. That way, it would appear that those of us left had nothing to do with Mama's schemes; we'd appear to be the victims. So that's the way it was, then ...

I felt a rustle around me as the air stirred. My grandmother was here, for when I closed my eyes, I could see red roses, her sign of love for me, and smell their scent surrounding me. My heart filled with joy to know she was around. Again, I heard her warning me *"Things aren't what they seem."*

CHAPTER 9

I slipped into the employee lounge and texted Brian to tell him not to come to the lounge that night because I had something I wanted to discuss with him and Mike at the house. Two seconds later he texted back "OK" and left it at that. Without waiting for a response, I texted Mike and told him to pick me up at the regular time.

Realizing the impossible situation Cindy and I were in, I had come up with an idea I thought might work to allow both Brian and Mike to get a better reception here at the lounge, and I wanted to discuss the idea of including Cindy in our investigation. We'd talk later.

It always was interesting to me that no matter what business closed its doors only to reopen them later, it created new excitement—and usually a line of people waiting to get in. The Purple Passion Lounge was no different. There was a flood of customers at 4 o'clock sharp, and then it slowed down for the rest of my shift, with just the regulars coming in.

Bambi came to relieve me at 7 p.m., and she was excited about seeing me. "Rosie, I'm so glad that you're back. I was worried you wouldn't be here because of all that'd happened. How are you?"

I smiled at her enthusiasm. "I'm fine, Bambi. It's good to see you too," I responded, holding out my arms to give her a hug.

I left her wearing a smile and headed to see Romano. The same red-faced, frustrated worker who had been in the kitchen earlier with a paintbrush was now trying to hang a beautiful print of a bowl of fruit on the wall to the left of the entrance.

"No, not there. Move it two inches to the left. That's almost it ... now move it back a tad. There, hold it right there, ordered Romano, elated. In a matter of minutes, the worker did what he had to do, stepped off the ladder, packed up everything, and left, obviously glad to be departing.

"I didn't know you were into art, Romano."

"Oh, my darling, any gay man worth his salt knows art," he responded with a twinkle in his eye.

I laughed with him as we eyed the artwork. "It's a beautiful print, Romano, really lovely. Who's the artist?"

"This is a print of a work done in the 1960s by G. Diehl. His style copies Cezanne's cubist still-life works. Nice, isn't it?"

I nodded in agreement, and because I couldn't wait any longer, I asked, "What do you having cooking today, Romano? Anything exciting?"

"Ah, my pet, it's always exciting to create. You know that with your writing, yes?"

I was taken aback, for I didn't realize he knew anything about me. When he saw my expression, he chuckled. "I'm very choosy who I allow into my kitchen, my darling Rosebud. It's only you and Cindy."

It was interesting it was just the two of us, but I was so very glad it was. I didn't actually know that much about Cindy, but if she passed Romano's inspection, there must be more to her than I realized. "Why, thank you, Romano. I feel so honored to be one of your chosen few," I teased.

"As well you should," he answered in a fake, fun tone. "Come and see what I've fixed for you."

This time his creation consisted of smothered pork, which in essence is pork boiled with sauerkraut and special seasonings. It became a one-pot meal when potatoes and carrots were thrown in for the last hour. It happened to be one of my favorite dishes, and I wondered whether he already knew that.

It soon was time for me to return to the front desk. I was feeling drained, and I was glad there were only a few hours left in my shift. Cindy arrived before it ended, and I was curious to find out more about her. We hugged, and I asked, "So, how are you doing? Are you okay?"

"I will be as soon as we straighten things out here."

"What exactly does 'straighten things out here' include?" I asked, my curiosity mounting.

Before she could answer, Mike arrived, and our conversation was cut short. "Hi, handsome," she called out.

Mike smiled and replied, "Hi there yourself."

I watched the two of them. Each was smiling, but I didn't sense a spark between them, or maybe it was that I didn't want to see one. Yet if Mike and Cindy became a serious couple, I'd be happy for them simply because I cared for them both. Besides, who doesn't want love in their life?

When I went to grab my purse from my locker, I took out my phone and texted Brian to tell him we were heading home now—did he still want to meet? When I returned to the front, Mike was standing close to Cindy, and she was whispering to him. I had no idea what they were discussing, but as soon as Mike saw me, he stepped back from her and said, "Ready?"

I hugged Cindy goodbye, and we left. Once in the car, Mike turned to me. "Did you have a good day?"

"I'm not sure 'good' is the right word. Interesting, for sure." On a whim, I asked, "Did Cindy fill you in?"

Mike looked a bit startled but simply answered, "Some."

"I texted Brian to see if he was available to meet with us. I've something I want to run by the two of you."

"Okay. I think we've got more to talk about anyway."

I wasn't sure what he meant, but I for one needed to dispel the nagging sense that *things weren't what they seemed.* That phrase had been ringing in my ear for the past couple of hours.

Although Sweet Pea was happy to see us, she was fairly calm, as if our arriving at this time of night were no longer new. She was adjusting. I put coffee on to brew, and Brian arrived as I laid out brownies on a plate. This time, Sweet Pea went crazy, and he could barely make it through the front door for all her bouncing around at his feet. He picked her up and came forward. "Ah, coffee's on, great."

As Brian joined Mike and me in the kitchen, I heard Mike whisper, "I think she knows."

Brian nodded his head.

I handed them each a cup of coffee and slid the plate of brownies onto the table, announcing, "I've got two things I want to run by you."

I sat down and began to tell them about the meeting Cindy and I had with Tony, Johnny, and Sylvia. I saw both of them flinch at the term "family," but they held back any response. I had their full attention now. "Here's what I propose we do. I've had the opportunity to observe Cindy, and I believe she can be trusted—she demonstrated that when she helped free the little girls. I think we need to consider having her join our investigation."

I watched both smile. Then Mike turned to Brian and said, "Guess it's your turn now."

Brian looked embarrassed. "Rosie, we've been holding something back from you because we didn't want it to taint how you would normally act in your job at the lounge ..."

I interrupted. "What you mean to say then, Cowboy, is that you felt you couldn't *trust* me?" I accused. "All that talk about us being a team, and you ..."

"Hold on, Rosie, you haven't even asked what that something is," interjected Mike.

"And you, Mike, you couldn't tell me either?"

"Wait just a minute, Rosie. Let's get to what we've been holding back from you—not why, all right?" asked Brian.

"You don't even have to bother. I know," I said in a smug voice.

"You do?" he responded.

"I got the message when I saw Mike whispering with Cindy tonight while he was there to pick me up."

"You did?" Mike asked.

The *'things aren't what they seem'* phrase that'd resounded in my head earlier made things very clear. "Cindy's already a part of our investigative team, isn't she?"

Both men looked like little boys who had been naughty. Finally, Brian said, "Yeah, you're right. Cindy's part of our investigative team."

"You two couldn't tell me before this?" Then I couldn't help myself. I looked at Mike and asked, "Is Cindy your girlfriend?"

He looked startled and didn't say anything for several seconds while both Brian and I waited eagerly for his response. All he said was "I don't have time for that." Then, quick to change the subject, he asked, "What's the second thing you wanted to discuss with us, Rosie?"

"Johnny's going to be watching Cindy and me very carefully. He's already expecting you, Mike, to be at the lounge because you're my boyfriend … supposedly," I added with emphasis. "As for you, Cowboy, Johnny doesn't like you there at all because he overheard Mike say you were interested in Bambi. She's someone he's keen on. However, if you could be Cindy's boyfriend, just like Mike and I are a couple, it'd help get you into the lounge as someone more than an irritating reporter with eyes on his girl. What do you guys think?"

Mike just smiled.

"No … I don't think that'll work," Brian muttered. "Me being her boyfriend and all. Do you think it's really a good idea?" he asked, looking directly at me.

"Of course I do. It makes all the sense in the world because it gives you a good reason to be there. You just need to loosen up a bit, that's all," I added, remembering his kisses on my forehead.

Mike began laughing. "You two."

"I'm sure Cindy will go along with it, don't you think, Mike?" I asked.

"It seems like a good idea to me. I think it'll be okay with her too. We just need to talk it over with her and see how she feels about it. Maybe we should go down there now for a nightcap, Brian. What do you think?"

"Sure, why not?"

I sat there dumbfounded by how quickly our three-way conversation turned into my sitting alone at the table with Sweet Pea at my feet staring at me. Her look seemed to question—is it something you said?

CHAPTER 10

T he next morning, I dressed in something a bit more suggestive than I'd worn yesterday. It was one of my fashion designer, Louie's, choices, and it made me feel more sophisticated than my usual wardrobe did. I needed something to perk me up, for I was feeling a bit low. Truth be told, I didn't really like working at the lounge, except for being with Romano and Cindy. In many ways, I found the place depressing, and the energy there so low that the time I spent there was draining.

As I came into the kitchen, Mike was standing in front of the sliding glass door looking out, deep in thought. When he heard me, he turned, and his face lit up. He stared at me for a few seconds, then slowly said in a low voice, "Wow, Rosie, you look beautiful."

"Thanks," I said indifferently. "So how was last night? Did Cindy agree to the plan?"

"Yes, she's a good sport. I knew she'd do whatever is necessary."

"So have you, Brian, and Cindy worked together for a long time?" I asked, a bit jealous of their time together.

"Not really. Just this past year."

Sweet Pea was scratching at the door to come in, so he slid it open. She ran to me and waited for me to give her a treat for being such a good girl.

"Would you like me to fix some scrambled eggs?" asked Mike.

"That would be great. Thanks."

As I waited for Mike to cook breakfast, I knew he could sense my dispirited mood. He came and stood behind my chair and rested his hand on my shoulder. "Rosie, you can't change the world overnight or fix all the wrongs in the way people treat each other. You have to take one day at a time. That's it. That's all there is to it."

My eyes watered. "You sound just like my grandmother." I chuckled as I saw his expression. "And I mean that in a good way. I sure do miss her."

And that was all it took for her to show up swirling around me. I closed my eyes and saw red roses for love and heard her say, *"It's going to be all right, Rosie. Hang in there."*

Mike was looking at me strangely. "Are you okay?"

I smiled with renewed energy, "I'm fine, Mike, really I am."

"Good," he said as he leaned down and kissed the top of my head.

I knew I was blessed to have these three people—Brian, Mike, and Cindy—in my life. We actually made a good team because we cared about and trusted each other—for the most part, I added.

I had ignored my writing, and I needed to complete my next assignment for the magazine, so after cleaning up the breakfast dishes, I went into my office, where I could write without interruption. I remembered what Mike had said earlier and decided my topic for the spiritual column would be understanding the importance of our role in life as an individual while at the same time acknowledging our role as part of the whole.

I lost myself in my writing until I heard the doorbell ring and Sweet Pea begin to bark. As I went to see who was at the door, my heart skipped a beat, for I wasn't expecting anyone. I could hear Mike upstairs, so I opened the door. I was surprised to see my next-door neighbor, Ron, standing there.

"Well, good morning, Ron."

"Good morning, Rosalie. Is your 'friend' still here?" he asked with some disapproval.

I felt myself blush. "Yes, Ron, he is. Why?"

"Do you think he'd be willing to help me with something?"

"Let's ask him. Mike?" I called.

He came charging down the stairs, and when he saw Ron, he looked surprised but greeted him with good cheer, "Hi there, neighbor."

"I was wondering if you could lend me a hand. I'm installing a new security system, and I need to mount several cameras on the roof. My wife won't let me do it alone—she's afraid I'll fall. I hate taking you away from anything, but ..."

Mike and I looked at each other and grinned. Ron's idea of "taking you away from anything" sounded much more exciting than it was. "No problem. Glad to help, Ron."

I watched them walk away and wondered why Ron suddenly felt he needed a security system, with cameras, no less. Maybe Mike would learn why he was doing this.

Several hours later, Mike came through the door chuckling. "Let me tell you, when Ron decides to do something, he sure does it in a big way."

"Any idea why he's installing this system now?"

"All he said was he wanted to make sure you were safe—that he'd promised your grandmother that."

Because I sensed him holding something back, I asked, "And?"

"He said you have too many men coming and going here at night. Your grandmother wouldn't like it."

"What he means is *he* doesn't like it, right?"

"Yup. Well, I'd better get cleaned up so I can drive you to work."

Too many men coming and going at night? Is there something going on that I don't know about? After all, there was really only Mike and Brian, right? Oh, and Thomas too, an employee of Brian's and Mike's company, who was working with us.

Mike dropped me off at the front door of the lounge. He gave me a quick kiss on the cheek and didn't bother to come in. Cindy was at the desk and seemed a bit disappointed that he hadn't. "Hi, Rosebud, how's it going?"

"Not too bad. How about you? What are you doing here?"

"Johnny called me in to give him a hand," she answered. "Guess you know, right? About me, I mean," she whispered. "We have lots to talk about now for sure."

"Are you okay with Brian being your boyfriend or a fiancé?" I asked.

"Well, we're just keeping it boyfriend for now." She chuckled. "I think Brian prefers it that way. He's a funny guy—they both are really. They like their freedom, that's for sure."

I thought she was probably right. A sudden thought came to me, and I mouthed, "Is Romano also working with us?"

Cindy laughed. She put her arm around my shoulders like chums do and whispered, "No. There's no way to keep him under the radar, if you know what I mean. He sure is a great guy though, isn't he?"

I had to agree with her on both counts—Romano was the best. "I'll just run to the employee lounge and be right back."

"You're way early, so take your time. Go have a cup of coffee with Romano if he's free. I'm fine here," she offered. Her schedule was way off. She was being a good sport, probably thinking she'd be able to put up with anything for a few days.

As I was on my way back to the employee lounge, I waved to Romano and yelled, "I'll be right back. Do you have time for me?"

He blew me a kiss and nodded. I knew we'd have a few minutes before I needed to be back up front. It certainly was comforting to have Romano as my friend, which made working at the lounge that much better. I quickly put my things into my locker, said hello to some girls I hadn't met yet, and hurried to the kitchen.

As I passed the partially closed door to one of the offices, I saw the same man I'd seen running away from where David Masterly's body had been floating in the lake; he was talking to Tony. I hurried past before he could see me, and I kept walking, hoping he'd remain in Tony's office. My radar was on high, and I could envision him at Lake Las Vegas struggling with David. Who was he? Was he responsible for David's death? Why?

As I stepped into the kitchen, Romano's greeting pulled me away from my thoughts. "Good afternoon, my little Rosebud. Would you care for a cup of tea? I'm steeping a fresh mint that is so …" he kissed his fingers, making me laugh.

I couldn't think of anything better at the moment and reached for one of the cookies from the plate he'd already laid out on the prep table. I was too enticed by the wonderful aroma and sweet taste of the cookies to worry about gaining any weight right now. "Romano? Do you know anything about the man who's meeting with Tony? Have you seen him before? He's a bit taller than you are, with dark brown hair, wearing a black baseball hat."

"I know who you mean. He tried to come in here and order me around earlier. I told him if he wanted anything from the kitchen, he'd have to have one of the girls out front wait on him like everyone else. He left, but he wasn't too happy."

"Do you know who he is?"

"Not really. I think he was a friend of David's, but I can't be sure. I've seen him around lately, that's all. Why?"

"Just wondering," I replied through a mouthful of cookie. "I'm also curious about how long you've been working here."

"Five years. Back then, I was down on my luck. I'd been hired as a sous chef at one of the large casinos here in Vegas, but it suddenly closed and was due to be torn down. I was desperate for a job, and my career counselor told me about this place that was just reopening. He told me, 'Just go in there for your interview and own the job.

That's the only way to do it. Then the job becomes yours.' And he was right."

"That's good advice for sure. You were lucky to have him as your counselor."

"It was the luckiest day of my life," he said with a smile spreading across his handsome face. "He's now my life partner." he crowed.

I chuckled, happy that things were good for him. When I thought about his having been here for five years, I wanted to know whether there was anyone working here now who'd been there then or before him. I knew that Sophia and her boss, Richard, were the original owners, but who else was still here? "So who hired you, Romano? Was it Sophia?"

When he heard her name, his eyes misted. He answered sadly, "She was a good woman, and I miss her visits here. We used to have tea together here."

When he saw my eyes had watered as well, he asked, "Did you know her?" Then he shook his head in exasperation, "Of course you did. You worked for her at PUP, didn't you?"

I nodded my head. "Romano, what can you tell me about her boss?"

"There's a story, for sure. I …"

Johnny stepped into the kitchen and simply said, "Time's up, Rosalie."

I jumped off my stool, gave Romano kisses, and headed to the front. I looked at my watch and was surprised to see it was already 4 o'clock, time for my shift to start. Where had the time gone?

CHAPTER 11

J ohnny was talking with Cindy when I reached the front; she looked serious and nodded her head in agreement at different points in their discussion. When they heard me come their way, they turned and faced me—Cindy with a smile, Johnny with an annoyed expression. Johnny said, "We've a slight change in plans for the next several days, Rosalie, and I expect your cooperation."

"All right," I agreed. "What do you need me to do?"

"Tony's cousin flies in tonight, and she'll want to start learning the ropes as soon as possible. I need you to come in two hours earlier for the next few days so you can be available to train her."

Did I have a choice? "Sure," I replied. I wasn't going to mention I wasn't scheduled for any time off in the near future, which was going to become a problem since I had no intention of working there seven days a week.

He looked at Cindy and said, "You'll come in two hours earlier for your shift too. I need you to continue to work with me to get David's office squared away so Tony's cousin can take it over." Cindy nodded her head in agreement. "C'mon, Cindy, let's finish up what we were working on," Johnny ordered.

As Johnny turned to leave, with Cindy following behind, she rolled her eyes at me and mouthed, "Damn."

As I watched them go, I knew Cindy had hoped to take over David's entire job, but now that wasn't likely to happen unless Tony's cousin couldn't handle it. Time would tell. "Hey, miss. I haven't got all day. Are you going to let me in or not?" demanded a low, gruff voice. Startled, I turned around, expecting a bully of a man, and found Brian standing there. In a lighter tone, he stated with pride, "Fooled you, didn't I?"

I had to agree. "Is Cindy around?" he asked enthusiastically. "She said she was here."

"Afraid not. She's off and running with Johnny. Anything I can help you with?"

"Naw, I guess not. I'm just trying to keep up appearances, that's all. Anything new here?"

"I've got a few questions. What do you know about who was involved here at the time the lounge changed its style of entertainment? Is there anybody from that time who's still here?"

"The usual suspects – the owners and management team - Tony, David, Bertha, Sophia, and Sophia's boss, Richard. Out of that list, we identified only Tony and Richard as owners, although we know Tony only represents one of them."

"And Sophia. You remember she was an owner as well?" I prodded him.

"Yes, of course. We're trying to find out who'll inherit her small portion. Haven't been able to do that yet."

"Maybe it goes back to Richard. He's the one who gave her the shares in the first place."

"Could be. You said before that you think David Masterly was B.B., right?"

"I think so, but I'm not so sure now. I just have a feeling it's not him."

"Why did you think it was David in the first place?"

"Well, first of all, we know someone with the initials B.B. was in love with Melissa, and she called David B.B., apparently for Big Boy, of all unlikely things."

Brian flushed. "You never know," was all he said.

"And guess what? I just found out Romano was hired here as chef just the week before the doors reopened and has remained here ever since."

"Good. He might be able to tell us stuff we wouldn't be able to dig up otherwise. See what you can find out, okay?"

"Sure. By the way, Tony's cousin is arriving tonight, so I'll have a chance to meet her. Cindy's helping to get David's office in order so the cousin can take it over. Cindy's very disappointed not to get that job straightaway, but you never know … ?"

"For sure," he agreed. "What's the cousin's name?"

"I've no idea. Someone from New Jersey, I think he said."

"Hmm." He looked at his watch and said, "Well, I'd better get going."

"Also, I'll be coming in here two hours earlier for my shift for the next few days. Johnny's orders."

Brian looked as if he were going to step toward me but instead immediately backed away, obviously remembering his role with Cindy.

"I'll tell Cindy you were here to see her," I said in a loud voice as Johnny turned the corner into the front area.

Johnny looked irritated by Brian's presence. I could tell Brian sensed it, for he tried to set things straight by stepping forward and formally introducing himself. "My name's Brian Boyce. I'm here to see Cindy."

"Cindy?"

"Yeah. My girlfriend, Cindy."

"Seems funny I didn't know that. Rosalie, run and get Cindy. Tell her she has a *surprise* out front."

At first, I didn't know whether Johnny was serious, but then he tipped his head in the direction of David's office. I took off, wondering how the two of them would work things out.

Cindy lit up when she saw me. "What're you doing here? Does Johnny know?"

"He's the one who sent me, believe it or not. It's supposed to be a surprise, but Brian's here to see you. I think Johnny is questioning whether your and Brian's relationship is real. Just be warned." I left her and scurried to the front.

Cindy arrived several minutes after me, and when she saw Brian she smiled wide. "Hi there, handsome, I'm so glad to see you." She marched forward and ran into Brian's arms, which he extended as she came closer. She planted a big kiss on his lips, and I was somewhat taken aback to see how he reciprocated. He was enjoying playing even more than the part of the boyfriend—more like the enamored lover. He reached low behind her and pulled her against him. My face reddened, and I turned away. Johnny looked at me, raised his eyebrows, and then walked away.

Cindy pulled away from Brian, saying, "That ought to show him."

Brian smiled, pleased. "I don't believe you left any doubt about that."

Cindy said, "See you two later. I've got to get back there before Johnny messes things up and I'm forced to stay longer." She turned to go and winked at me as she passed.

Brian was so satisfied with what had just taken place that I became completely annoyed. Before I could go further with that thought, a customer came in, demanding quick service to register and get into the bar area. He looked as if he'd been drinking already, which might cause problems later. I'd have to alert Johnny.

Brian stood and watched me for the few minutes it took me to sign the man in. Afterward he teased, "See you later, alligator."

Instead of responding "In a while, crocodile," I just looked at him and said nothing.

"Or maybe not," he added and walked out the door, whistling. He knew I was annoyed and most likely why. I can't always hide my emotions as much as I might like. There it was again—that ole push-me-pull-you thing we had going between us. Remember, I chastised myself, putting Brian and Cindy together was your idea.

Just before my break, a rather nice-looking woman about my age walked in. She had wild, dark hair to her shoulders and wore oversized sunglasses and leopard-patterned clothing, which looked a bit cheap. There was a large gold leather purse hanging from her shoulder. Looking behind her, she turned to our valet, who was dragging her three large suitcases along, and ordered, "Just leave my bags here. Tony can take them from here."

She had a very distinct New Jersey accent, which made me smile. Obviously, Tony's cousin had arrived.

Oblivious to me for the moment, she looked around at all the gray marble and said in a low voice, "Well, it's not as tacky as I thought it'd be." I watched her with interest as she went to one of the new fake plants and touched its leaves. "Not bad," she said. Then she saw me behind the desk and asked, "And who are you?"

I smiled and replied, "My name's Rosalie."

"Ahh. I've heard about you and what you did. Smart girl."

I didn't know what to say, because I wasn't sure what she meant by "smart girl" or whether that was good or bad—or even what it referred to. Her voice sounded a bit odd, almost as if all the words were said in the same tone, with little modulation. She came forward saying, "Where are my manners? My father says I lost them a long time ago, and I believe he might be right," she ended with a chuckle. "My name's Mary Margaret. Just call me Mimi for short."

There was something about her I immediately liked. I knew we were going to get along just fine.

The valet had obviously let Tony know his cousin was here, for he came around the corner and with fake pleasure said, "Well, Mimi, here, at last." Tony managed to make his comment sound like a reprimand, and Mimi was not about to let that stand.

"Well, cousin, it took you long enough to leave your office to greet me. Get my bags, and show me where my quarters are in this joint."

I ducked down and pretended I was busy and had not heard their conversation. Tony could be vindictive, and I didn't want him to retaliate in any way because

I'd overheard Mimi's harsh treatment of him. I smiled to myself. Yes, I certainly was going to enjoy having Mimi here.

CHAPTER 12

Bambi came to take over so I could take my break, and I couldn't wait to get to Romano's kitchen. I was anxious to ask him questions—plus, I was starving. "Hey there, my sweet Romano," I called to him. We air-kissed, and then he grasped my shoulder, gently pushing me forward toward a seat at the end of the prep table.

"Wait here, Rosebud. I'll be right back."

I was so lucky to have Romano fuss over me, and I didn't think it'd be possible to ever tire of his waiting on me. Besides, it was always fun to try to guess what he had in store for me to eat. It was usually something different each time. When he returned, he handed me a wonderful BLT sandwich, one of my favorites, with fresh-cut apple slices on the side. Then he sat beside me for our time together. I don't know which of us enjoyed this time more, and it was as if we'd known each other all our lives, which made it very comfortable to be together. Between mouthfuls, I asked, "Have you met Mimi yet?"

"Is that Tony's cousin? No, not yet."

"I think you're going to like her."

"Well, we'll see. As long as she stays out of my kitchen and doesn't make too many demands, we'll get along just fine."

As if we had fabricated her, Mimi blew into the kitchen. "Hi there, so you're the chef everyone raves about. I'm Mimi. I have a feeling you and I are going to get along just fine for as you can see, I love to eat," she said while patting her slightly rounded belly.

It was amusing to watch Romano, for it was easy to see he was torn between not wanting an uninvited guest in his kitchen and loving her obvious sweet talk about his cooking. Soon flattery won him over. "Ah, a girl after my heart. Well, you'll have a chance to see for yourself. Send in one of the girls, and I'll have her serve you something delicious."

"Not here?" she asked, eying me sitting there.

"No, my lady," he stated emphatically, "Just send in one of the girls, and I'll fix you up in no time."

I was uncomfortable sitting there watching Mimi being dismissed by her company's chef, but she didn't seem fazed by Romano's treatment. Good-naturedly, she simply said, "No problem. Just no dessert for me, please," as she once again patted her belly before walking out.

Romano and I looked at each other and grinned. I said, "See, I told you so. I think she's going to be okay." I took another bite of my sandwich and asked, "What do you know about her family? Anything?"

Romano was relishing the role of storyteller. "First of all, do you know who her father is?" he asked smugly.

As I shook my head no, he continued, "He's a big businessman in New Jersey, very successful, though I'm not exactly sure what business he's in. Some say he's part of the Mafia back there. At any rate, he's made a lot of money. He has just the one child—that's Mimi, of course."

"Is that the owner Tony represents?"

"Yes, and it's also Mimi's father who brought Mama here. Mama is his niece by marriage, and she and Mimi are cousins, though not that close in age." He paused, then continued. "Mama's stepfather and Mimi's father were brothers. But most people don't know that because Mama and her brother were adopted by the brother's wife before they married, and they don't share the family name."

Romano paused once more, trying to pull together additional facts. Then he added, "Sophia told me that Mama's stepfather was once a bigwig in the Mafia but was killed when he got too greedy. It happened when Mama was just a teenager, and basically, she and her family were left penniless. She's never gotten over it and tries to bully everyone into thinking she's still part of the Mafia, although most people involved don't consider her to be. That is, according to Sophia. Follow me so far?"

Boy, did I ever! "Things are beginning to make sense now," I said as I carried my dishes to the sink. As I looked up at the clock, I saw I'd have to hurry to get back in time to relieve Bambi. "Romano, you are the best. Ciao, baby." This time we blew each other kisses as I ran out of the kitchen.

I made it with just seconds to spare and found Bambi standing behind the desk, looking a bit frazzled. "What's wrong, Bambi?" I asked with concern.

"Mimi doesn't think I'm old enough to be behind the desk. She likes someone older—more your age," she whined. I had to laugh to myself, for unless you were under 20, these young girls here considered you old.

"Well, maybe it's for the best," I said. "You'd rather be out there dancing anyway, right?"

That seemed to perk Bambi up a bit, making her smile. "Yeah, you're right. Better tips for sure too," she laughed.

She hugged me and ran off, which made me wonder whether that meant only Cindy and I would be assigned to the front desk going forward. How was that going to work? Would we ever get a day off?

When Cindy joined me at the end of my shift, she looked more refreshed than I had seen her that afternoon, proving once again even a few hours of sleep makes a difference. As always, I was glad to see her. "I've got some news about Mama," I whispered, as I hugged her.

"Spill, girl, let's hear it," she whispered back.

We were always careful not to speak in a loud voice when we were up front because we suspected there might be hidden microphones. After I filled her in, her response was what I'd said earlier—"Now it's beginning to make sense."

She looked through the one-way window to make sure we had no guests coming in. Then she turned her back to the front and stood by my side, adding, "When I was going through David's things, I found an old photo of what must have been Mama, and it had the name Bertha Beauman written on the back. Let me tell you, when she was young, she was a real looker, I mean *really* beautiful. I don't know what happened, but she sure doesn't look like that now."

"Maybe that's what unhappiness does to you."

"For sure," responded Cindy.

We turned in time to see both Mike and Brian come through the door. Brian grabbed Cindy at the same time

Mike pulled me to him. The four of us laughed together because it was just for show. Mike said, "I think I'll join Brian for a drink. What do you say, want to join us?"

I looked at Cindy, who raised her shoulders as if to say it was up to me.

"Am I allowed to?" I asked her.

"Sometimes, after my shift, I've joined Mike or Brian and no one has said anything, so why not?"

That's interesting, I thought. I should've realized that the three of them met from time to time to talk things over. "Sweet Pea is settled in for the night, isn't she?" I asked. Mike nodded his head in affirmation. "Okay, then. Let's go."

I felt awkward entering the bar where the stage with its dancing pole was positioned in the middle, exposed to all areas of the room. It was difficult to ignore the girls dancing there and anything that was happening at one of the tables. For the most part, things seemed calm and respectful in spite of the noise of the music and a lone whistle call. I knew as soon as anything got out of hand, Johnny or one of the security guards would quietly escort the offender out of the bar and lounge entirely.

We chose a table in a more quiet location farthest from the center of the lounge, where two girls had paired up to perform and had drawn the attention of nearly everyone in the room. Mike smiled at me. "What's happenin' darlin'?"

I could feel Brian perk up at Mike's calling me darling, but he simply asked, "So, what's new?"

I filled them in on Mimi, telling them there was something about her I liked. I didn't think she fit in with all that was going on here and sensed there'd soon be some changes made. "How about you two? Anything new?"

105

"We're still waiting for the autopsy report on David Masterly to see if there are any ties to the other deaths," replied Brian. "Channel 5 news is trying to keep a low profile on his case, even though I was the one to call in the story. Other than that, I'm kept busy doing regular boring reporter work. That boss of mine has found more crazy stuff for me to follow up on that never gets mentioned on the air. He's amazing that way. He doesn't leave me much time during the day to get everything done I'd like to," he said with frustration.

"How about you, Mike?" I asked.

"I'm following up on the list of men who were here that night for the auction of the girls. It's interesting that some of them were simply substitutes sent here to do the bidding for the actual buyers. And they're not talking, so it's going to take a bit longer to fit all the pieces together. I also have to believe those little girls weren't the buyers' firsts." He sighed. "We know that Phoenix is the number one place for human trafficking, but if we're not careful, Las Vegas will be close behind."

"I was thinking of checking in with the girls tomorrow to make sure they're okay," I said. "The oldest one speaks a tiny bit of English, and I think she'll talk to me."

"Good," Mike responded. "They wouldn't allow me to see them where they're staying right now. They said the girls are too traumatized and terrified of any man at this point."

"Well then, tomorrow I'll make an appointment to see them as soon as possible. I'll try to get there sometime before I have to leave for work," I said.

"Sounds good," interjected Brian.

"Where's your mystery man in all this?" I asked.

Mike looked to Brian for his response, for he was curious as well. "He's leaving it up to the four of us to get things straightened away. Mama is out on bail, as you know, and he wants us to keep an eye on her. All the top-notch lawyers are working to exonerate Tony and Johnny, saying it was all Mama's doing. David, of course, doesn't count in all of this not only because he's dead but also because anyone looking at him would know he couldn't have pulled this off. He was Mama's puppet, and both Tony and Johnny confirmed that."

"What's happening on the drug end?"

"That's a different story. We know that Johnny and Tony are involved, but we can't prove it. Again, they are letting Mama take the fall. However, we'll see what happens. I heard there's going to be a preliminary hearing sometime soon, within the next few weeks or so."

"It's interesting how things get slowed down in the court system, isn't it?"

"Yup," Mike said, while Brian nodded his head in agreement.

I was tired. I looked at Mike and asked, "Ready to go home?" It sounded so natural coming from my lips that it took my breath away.

Mike's eyes twinkled as he played along. "Awright, honey, let's go home." He pulled me from my chair. "Are you all set here, Brian?"

"Yeah. Cindy's break is coming up soon, and I'll fill her in on what we've discussed. You two go on. I'll see you both tomorrow."

"Sounds good," I added and bent to give Brian a kiss on the cheek. He looked surprised—but not as surprised as Mike. I mouthed, "Just playing the game."

It had been a long day. They were only going to get longer with my added hours. Mike and I waved to Cindy, who was tending to a customer as we walked by. Then Mike turned back and called to her, "Brian's waiting for you inside. See you tomorrow?"

She smiled. "Okay."

Tomorrow would indeed be another day, God willing.

CHAPTER 13

I woke up feeling something big was going to happen, though I had no clue what it'd be. I made a quick list of things I wanted to accomplish before work. At the top of my list was to make contact with the little girls so I could see for myself they were okay. I had dreamed of them last night, and I knew they had something to tell me.

Sweet Pea ran up the stairs, searching for me. Obviously, Mike had tended to her, and she was wondering why I was taking so long to join them in the kitchen. I looked at her and realized that if all little girls were treated as well as I cared for my dog, their lives would be very good. Instead, many times girls were treated as mere things to be used for pleasure by men. I recognized that in some aspects we all are animals, creatures in a pecking order, and that it was up to us to protect those who were unable to protect themselves. There was no way these little girls deserved to be treated with less respect and love than we'd want for ourselves. Who were these men who believed differently and were willing to buy them? Hadn't we had enough of that in the past with the auctioning of slaves? When was this kind of behavior going to end?

I needed to find out more about what I and others could do to save girls (and boys too) from human trafficking. It was too early for me to make any telephone calls, so I grabbed my robe and headed downstairs for the cup of coffee I knew was waiting for me. I felt too lazy to tend to my hair, and I didn't care that it was all over the place. Maybe I'd reach out to the hairdresser Louie had suggested to see how he'd deal with it. I knew my hair would be a challenge for anyone.

Mike took one look at me and didn't say a word but puttered around the kitchen until he noticed I had finished my first cup of coffee. He was good about allowing me space to face the day. "Rosie, I've got surveillance tonight. Do you think you'll be okay here alone for a few hours tonight, or should I call in someone else?"

I sat straight up in my chair, fully alert, wondering why he'd even asked. "Of course, why wouldn't I be?" Goose bumps ran across my arms.

"I'm just making sure you're okay with it. Brian wants you well protected, and we both need to know you're safe."

It was gratifying to know that they were concerned about me. However, it was a little disquieting to realize how easy it had become to be dependent on someone else after just a short time of the routine. Truth be told, it would seem a bit lonely without Mike, but it would do me no good to think he'd always be here with me. Did I even want that?

Once we solved the murders, would I ever see either of them again?

After breakfast, I made my call to the agency that was keeping the girls safe. After I explained who I was and what I wanted, they seemed pleased I'd contacted them. They told me the oldest girl had asked for me, and they asked whether I'd be able to visit that morning. They gave me directions to a place that wasn't part of their organization but was more like a safe house. They warned me to come alone because they didn't want to draw any attention to the girls' location and have it identified. I was glad they were safe where they were—for the moment, at least.

I rushed to get dressed and told Mike where I was going and that I'd be back in a couple of hours. As I pulled out of the driveway, I saw Ron outside, and I returned his wave. I was lucky to have him as a neighbor, even if he was a bit nosy.

My thoughts were on the girls, speculating about what they might have to say. I checked my rearview mirror and saw that a car that had pulled in behind me a mile or so back was still behind me. Was someone following me? A chill ran through my body, and I knew this wasn't good.

I made a quick turn into a shopping mall as though that were my destination. The car followed me. I decided not to park in the parking garage, which I knew made me vulnerable without other people around; instead, I looked for an outdoor space close to the entrance of the mall. I was in luck, and when I saw a car pull out of a perfect parking spot, I grabbed it. I immediately jumped out to run inside the mall, where I stood inside the glass doors and looked back to see whether I could make out the driver through the dark glass of his car windows as he passed. Nothing.

I stayed there waiting for a glimpse of him, and just as I thought perhaps he'd decided to leave, I saw a man I recognized hurrying toward the entrance—it was the same man who'd run past me along the trail at Lake Las Vegas, the same man I believed had something to do with David Masterly's death. I immediately ran into the first store I came to and found myself in Victoria's Secret. Ignoring my desire to poke through the elegant bras and panties on display, I raced to the far back and into a dressing room before either of the salespeople even looked my way.

It wasn't too long afterward that I heard a sweet voice ask, "Sir, is there anything I can help you with?"

"I'm looking for my girlfriend," a gruff voice responded. "She said to meet her here."

"I'm sorry, but there's no one here."

"She's got to be here, she couldn't have gotten too far. Search all the dressing rooms," he ordered.

"I'm telling you, there's no one here," argued the sales clerk.

"Listen, if you don't check them, I will. Understand me?"

By this time, the manager had overheard enough to know trouble was brewing. She stepped in. "Sir? I'm the manager. Just what's the problem?"

"I'm looking for my girlfriend. I know she's here."

The clerk whispered to her manager, "He said she couldn't have gotten too far." They looked at each other and said nothing.

"I'm telling you you'd better check the dressing rooms, or I will," he demanded again.

"No problem, sir. Just step back and out of the way, please."

"Did you want to look at these pretty little panties she might enjoy wearing just for you?" asked the sales clerk, holding these in his face, obviously trying to draw his attention away. "Or what about these bras?"

I was tucked into the corner of the first dressing room, squatting on the bench so my feet wouldn't show below the door. As the manager swung open my door, I put my finger to my lips. She gave a slight nod of her head and continued down the rest of the row of dressing rooms, slamming open the doors as if in anger. "No one here, sir."

"But ..."

"Good day, sir," she said in a tone of dismissal—and I heard him walk away.

After a short time, I emerged from the dressing room and gave both ladies a hug. "Thank you so much."

The manager said, "That man certainly is up to no good. I'm going to call security right now. And don't worry, we're not going to use your name or description," she added. "That's what you want, isn't it?"

As I nodded in agreement, the sales clerk warned, "You'd better stay away from him if you know what's best for you."

"I couldn't agree more. Thank you ladies for everything."

True to her calling, the sales clerk asked, "Is there anything I can show you before you go?"

All three of us laughed. I hurried to my car so I wouldn't keep the girls waiting.

CHAPTER 14

T he house where the girls were staying was unremarkable and looked like most of the others in the neighborhood, and like them, it had a backyard enclosed in cement blocks for privacy. As I headed to the front door, I thought I heard water splashing and realized the house probably had a pool in the back for the girls to play in.

An older woman opened the door and led me into a good-sized living room. It had a large window through which we could see the pool outside and the four girls swimming and smiling as the oldest one splashed them and said something in Spanish. I smiled, and the woman observed my obvious enjoyment of watching them play together.

"The girls are happy now, but at night they cry," she said in despair.

My heart leapt at the thought of their distress. "How can I help?"

She held her hand out, "My name's Maria. I'm glad you've come. The oldest one repeats your name at night. She first calls you Rosie, and then she calls you Mama. I know she'll be glad to see you. C'mon, let's go outside to say hello."

As I started forward, I suddenly stopped and looked back at Maria and confessed, "I don't even know their names. Will you please introduce us?"

Maria seemed surprised but nodded in agreement. When I turned to the open glass slider, I felt wet arms surround my waist and looked down into the face of the oldest girl, the first one I'd seen at the lounge. Tears were rolling down her face, and she softly repeated, "Mama" as she clung to me. I wrapped my arms around her, and my eyes filled. I was overcome with a sadness I had never known before.

The other girls climbed out of the pool and came forward, shyly reaching out to touch me. One of them said, "Loca," and they all giggled, even the girl still enclosed in my arms.

Maria only half-heartedly scolded in Spanish, "You mustn't call anyone crazy—it's not polite."

They looked at her for a moment, then shook their heads in denial. They pointed at me, saying once again, "Loca." We realized at that moment their name for me would always be Loca. I laughed and pulled them to me in a group hug. "Now, I want to know *your* names."

Maria helped me. "This one is the youngest one, only nine years old; her name is Mariana. The next two are 10- year-old twins, Luciana and Valentina. The girl you're holding onto is 11, and her name is Isabella."

I looked at each of them and said, "What beautiful names you have. They suit you perfectly, as they're as beautiful as you are."

I wasn't sure they understood what I'd said, but they smiled anyway. "Isabella? Do you have something you want to tell me?" I asked. Maria translated.

She stepped away and looked up at me, nodding her head. "Bad people. Danger. Not safe for you."

As I took that in, Maria translated what Isabella added— "Things aren't what they seem." I felt my strength drain, making me weak in my knees. It was only my resolve to keep standing that kept me upright.

"Those aren't her exact words, but that's the best I can translate it into English," added Maria.

Isabella grabbed me and babbled words in Spanish. "What did she say?" I asked Maria, as the little girl's grip tightened around me.

Maria looked a bit embarrassed. "She says she doesn't want to stay here, she wants to go home with you. She says you are her real mama now."

I was speechless. My thoughts traveled back to the time of my mother's death; I'd been close to Isabella's age, and I'd been blessed to have my grandmother step in to become my loving mother figure. Who did this little girl have in her life to do the same? Worry filled me. "I thought your agency was locating their families and sending them back." Then it was my time to blush with embarrassment as I really wasn't that naïve.

Maria looked sad. "Sometimes we are lucky enough to do that, but most times, that's not the way it works, particularly if they come from a different country. The twins are very fortunate because their parents reported them missing as soon as they were taken. They'll head back to Mexico in a few days."

"What will happen to Marianna and Isabella?" I asked with panic in my voice.

"We're still working on finding some of their relatives. We have a whole network we work through. Time will tell."

I looked into Isabella's eyes and held them. I was hopeful I'd be able to transmit the message that I'd never let harm come to her if I could help it. My hands were tied, for I was in no position to take on a child at this point in my life. It wouldn't be the best for her either, for I really knew nothing about children. "Isabella, I need you to stay here with Maria where it's safe. With me, you'd be in harm's way. I can't have that, do you understand?"

Maria translated, and Isabella pulled away, furious with me and her circumstances, though I knew she was smart enough to know what I'd said was true. I added, "You have to trust me, Isabella. I'll see that everything gets done to connect you with your family again."

At hearing that, Isabella shook her head back and forth in irritation, "No, not there. With you." she called over her shoulder.

I looked helplessly at Maria as we watched Isabella march away in frustration. "I don't even know what to say," I said. "What can I do to help her?"

"I don't know. Perhaps you could pay for a private investigator, but you really need to talk to the agency to see what they have to say. I have their number right here. Let me get it for you."

I left, unhappy with the situation Isabella was in. I had gotten a clear sense that putting her back with her family was not right for her, yet who was I to judge?

118

When I arrived home, I was not in a good frame of mind. I was grateful Sweet Pea was there to greet me, but it was Mike I wanted to talk to. He was gone, though he'd left me a note saying he was working on his part of our investigation and wouldn't be available. This also was his night for surveillance, which meant I'd have no contact with him later either. I sighed. I'd have to be on guard tonight because I'd gotten careless with Mike as my protector.

I dressed for work, not particular about what I put on; however, with Louie's wardrobe choices, I knew I'd look good anyway. I sat with Sweet Pea on my lap so I could spend a little private time with her. I told her this day was going to be a long one for her, and I made sure she had plenty of water, food, and treats. I turned on the lights for when it got dark; she probably wouldn't care whether they were on, but I did.

I needed to clear my head and went into my office, where I sat down to meditate for a few minutes before I left for work. When I closed my eyes and began to relax, I immediately saw a vision of Richard arguing with Tony. It was so real that I jumped up from my chair and knocked over the tarot cards on my desk. I groaned as I saw the cards in a heap on the floor, with just one card—the Death card—showing. No surprise, really.

CHAPTER 15

I was in no mood to be at work that day, especially since the Death card had reared its ugly head again. However, despite my reluctance, I got to work just in time to be two hours early, as requested. I hurried to the employee lounge to put my purse away before meeting with Mimi. It seemed odd to see no one in the public areas, especially the bar area, and it was ghostly quiet.

As I made my way down the hall to the employee lounge, I heard intense arguing further down the hall and footsteps coming toward me at a fast pace from the pool area. I was too far away from the employee lounge to make it there without anyone seeing me, but I desperately didn't want to get involved in their argument. Instinctively, I turned into the office closest to me so I could hide and they'd walk on by without realizing I was near. I looked around the room and saw a closet with a louvered door, and instinct told me to step inside for added security. The sound of their steps kept coming closer and closer, while their voices became louder and louder. I recognized Tony's voice, but I wasn't sure who the other person was.

Instead of going farther down the hall, they stopped at the doorway of the office where I was hiding. Tony opened the door wide, and he and another man stood just inside the entrance way. I peeked through the slats of the louvered door, and saw that the other person was Richard, Sophia's boss and partner. He and Tony stood facing each other with Richard closer to me.

Richard's face was all red, and spittle was flying. "You've no right to do all the lousy things you've done to put *me* in great danger without my consent. And for God's sake, why Sally, of all people? You know she didn't have anything to do with those missing papers, yet you had her killed. I know it was you, you bastard. For Chrissake, she was your cousin. Have you no respect for family?"

"Just because you were in love with her, old man, doesn't mean she was innocent." Reacting to the look of incredulity on Richard's face, Tony defended himself. "Besides I didn't have her killed—you've got to believe me on that score. I tell you, I *didn't* kill her."

"Then who did? Tell me who did, you lying bastard."

"Listen to you, you old fool. Who do you think you're talking to anyway?" Tony asked, trying to puff himself up.

"I'm talking to a little sleaze ball fucker, that's who I'm talking to. You and B.B.—what a pair you two make. You deserve each other. I hope you all rot in hell, where you belong."

Richard stood there a moment with an odd expression on his face and weighed his words. "I've had it with all of

you and what you stand for. I should've never trusted ..."
He reached into his pocket and pulled out a gun.

"I wouldn't do that if I were you," interrupted Johnny, who had just appeared in the doorway.

"What have I got to lose? Sophia's dead, and so is Sally. Do you honestly think my life is worth anything knowing what we've been involved in?" Before anyone could react, Richard raised the gun to his head and shot himself. Both Tony and Johnny wore a look of stunned surprise and horror on their faces as they watched him crumble to the floor. In unison, they said, "Fuck."

This had all taken place in a matter of seconds, and I was trying not to gag or make any sound at all. I'd never seen anything like that, but it was everything sad and awful that has ever been written about it. I prayed that I wouldn't be discovered. Blood and bits of brain had spattered my way but I didn't dare look down to see if any was on me.

I felt a swirl of my grandmother's spirit surrounding me, but then an odd thing happened. I swear I heard her speak to the two men frozen in the doorway. *"Shut the door and immediately go change your clothes before you do anything else."*

I saw them stare at each other. As Tony began to close the door, I heard him say, "Johnny, we'd better get cleaned up and change before we deal with this mess. Just don't let anyone see you."

I listened as heavy footsteps hurried down to the several private apartments close to the pool area. I stifled my tears as I opened the closet door, and I gagged as I tiptoed around the body, being careful about where I stepped. I had to make sure none of my footprints would ever be found there. I peeked around the door to make sure no one was around, then slipped into the ladies' bathroom and locked the door. I looked down to see a small spatter of blood on my pant leg and lower shin and several on my shoes, which I must have picked up while I removed myself from the closet and office area. I could easily wash away the one on my pant leg and skin, but the shoes were a different story. They were leather with suede straps that seemed to have soaked up the bloody bits. Even if I were able to remove them, the suede would look odd because it'd require rough handling to clean them up. And because I was wearing cropped pants, my shoes—and anything on them—would show.

I looked in the mirror and hardly recognized my face. Mascara and tears were running down my cheeks, and I looked terrible. I scolded myself, saying out loud, "You need to get a grip, Rosalie Bennett, and pull yourself together right now." As I removed my makeup kit from my purse, I noticed my moisturizer and had an idea. I immediately opened the jar and applied the cream to the suede straps of my shoes, which smoothed the suede and made it all the same color. I was pleased with the result, for unless someone was intent on my shoes, no one would be the wiser.

I reapplied my makeup, unlocked the door, and scooted toward the employee lounge. As I neared it, I could hear Tony and Johnny coming toward me, and they appeared surprised to see me. "I'm so sorry I'm late," I gushed. "I apologize for not getting here on time. I promise it won't happen again."

Neither one spoke for several seconds, almost as if they had forgotten I was to come in early. Johnny was the first to react. "See that it doesn't happen again, hear?" As they began to realize that meant I wasn't around when Richard killed himself, expressions of relief washed over their faces before each of us went our own way.

I entered the employee lounge and collapsed against the closed door with a sense of relief. *"Gram,"* I whispered, *"Thank you so much for helping me out."* I felt her love surround me, and it was hard to halt the tears that threatened to begin again. I didn't know how I was going to get through my shift without anyone noticing I wasn't myself.

I popped in to say a quick hello to Romano, who blew me kisses and called out, "Come back later, my sweet Rosebud. I can't talk now. I'm in the middle of pulling together this new recipe and can't stop midway."

Mimi was not at the front desk when I got there, so I took a breather, sat down with my eyes closed, and began to meditate. I realized then I hadn't texted or phoned Cindy, Brian, or Mike about Richard's death. The more I thought about it, the happier I was I hadn't. It would be best to just let things unfold naturally, and when the news came out, I'd pretend to be as shocked as everyone else.

Suddenly, I felt a light touch on my shoulder. Startled, I looked up to see Mimi smiling at me. "Tough day already?"

As I returned her smile, I thought she'd know soon enough just how tough it's been. It'd be interesting to see how she'd handle the latest catastrophe at the lounge. "Sorry about that. Ready to begin?" I asked.

"Sure, as ready as I'll ever be, I guess."

I felt a little foolish showing her just how little brainpower this job required. Both of us knew I was there because of my looks. "This job is really simple routine work, especially since Sylvia does the actual accounting."

"Ah, yes, Sylvia," was Mimi's only response.

My next comment just spilled out. "I couldn't help but notice the software we're using is a bit outdated. There are others that allow you to handle more information, particularly if you want the transactions to be automatically coded into any of the current financial software."

Mimi looked at me in surprise. "Does that mean there'd be no need for Sylvia?"

"Not at all. It simply gives you a greater system of checks and balances."

"Ahh," was all Mimi said for a moment. "Maybe we should look into that."

I showed her what I meant so she could see for herself. She asked some questions about using Square as means for payments to have the money go directly into a bank account. I blurted what had occurred to me without my thinking about it. "You might want to check that account."

Mimi studied me. "Maybe I will. Tony looks at me simply as someone to appease because of his ties with my father, so I let him think I'm dumb. When I was in college, he was away by then and forgets that I've a double degree in finance and business administration."

She was dumb all right—dumb as a fox. "Are you going to be here long?" I asked, then laughed with her. "That sounded funny and not at all how I meant it. Please excuse me."

"Not at all. My father is having me evaluate whether it's worth it to keep this place open. He wants me to …"

Johnny, who still looked frazzled in spite of being neat as a pin in fresh clothing, interrupted us. "Come quickly, Mimi, come now."

Johnny turned to me and ordered, "You stay put here and don't move."

Mimi got up from her chair. "What's going on?"

"We've got a problem we need you to handle. Come with me."

CHAPTER 16

By now, it was past time for my break, but I didn't dare move. So far, no one had come to relieve me, and I hadn't heard any wild screaming or carrying on while Mimi had been away from the front desk. I had no idea what was going on, and my curiosity was mounting.

Bambi appeared out of nowhere, wearing her cover-up. "Johnny sent me to take over for your break. He said for you to take your full time."

Curious to know if she'd heard or seen anything, I asked, "What's happening, Bambi, anything exciting?"

She leaned forward and whispered, "Something's definitely going on around here, but I'm just not sure what. Johnny has blocked off the back hall. If you need anything from your locker, too bad."

"Thanks for the warning," I responded, sincere in not wanting to upset anything by heading to the employee lounge. Making calls to Cindy, Brian, or Mike would have to wait. I'd go see Romano; maybe he'd know what was happening.

"Ah, my little Rosebud, I'm glad you've come. I've made the most delicious new recipe, and I want to see what you think of it."

Apparently, Romano was not in the know about anything that happened at the lounge if it didn't take place in his kitchen. I was disappointed I'd learn nothing more. I grinned at Romano, saying, "I've got to be the luckiest girl in the world to be here with you right now." He didn't know how true that statement was, for me to be standing there with him, instead of dealing with Tony and Johnny as a witness to Richard's suicide.

Of course, the meal was fabulous. It was baked chicken breast with a honey-mustard sauce placed on sweet black rice, served with steamed broccoli. Romano sat on a stool next to me and told me how easy it was to make the sauce that topped the chicken. Then he glanced down, and my heart began to thump when I saw he was examining my shoes. He bent down, touched one of the straps, and immediately pulled his hand away. It came up red with dye from the shoe. He practically squealed, "What have you done with your shoes? It feels like they have grease on them."

Leave it to him to notice, I thought. My heart sank until I realized nobody but Romano would be interested in my shoes, and that, most likely, was only because of our proximity. I wasn't sure he'd buy my response, but I said, "I just wanted to smooth down the suede to make it match the rest of the shoe."

"Well, darling, it's not working. You've red dye on your legs now."

I looked down, and sure enough, I had red marks from the straps around my ankles. "Oh, my god, what am I going to do?"

"You, my little Rosebud, are going to sit right there while I grab some alcohol so I can get you and your shoes cleaned up."

I started to panic. Had anyone else noticed? I was pretty sure Bambi hadn't, and no one from the bar area had paid any attention to me when I passed around it. As my breathing became ragged with stress, Romano stood staring at me. "You're in trouble, aren't you?"

I didn't know what to say, so I simply nodded. I squelched the tears that threatened. "But I'm okay now."

"You can always talk to me, you know," he said soothingly.

As I remained silent, swallowing tears, he turned away with my shoes in hand. He hurried back with a rag with alcohol on it and handed it to me before he strode away again. As best I could, I wiped the dye from my legs, but it wasn't easy to tell the difference between the dye and the pink of my skin after I rubbed so hard.

When he returned, Romano's expression was grim. "I think I've cleaned them up as well as I can. There was some other stuff on the shoes as well, and I'm pretty sure it was blood. Are you okay?"

As I was slipping my shoes back on, Johnny appeared. "Times up, Rosalie."

When he saw what I was doing, he had an inquisitive expression on his face. Without hesitation, I said, "Romano gives a great foot massage."

Johnny looked at Romano, whose face was blank, and said, "I'll have to remember that," before he turned away and left.

Romano was wearing a grin. "As a matter of fact, I do. My partner says my foot massages are the best he's ever had." Turning serious, he whispered, "I'll keep all this between us. I'd never do anything to harm you, my darling girl. Just know that."

Instead of air-kissing him, I moved closer and planted big kisses on both his cheeks. "Romano, you are absolutely the best. I'm indebted to you for everything you do for me, especially for protecting me."

He flushed with pleasure, and I turned and left, filled with sadness.

Bambi was in a hurry to get back to dancing and didn't stay to talk. More important, she hadn't noticed my pink ankles or my freshly cleaned shoes. I sat down with relief and watched through the front one-way window as a patrol car and an ambulance pulled around to the back of the building without any sirens. So that's how Mimi's going to handle this, I thought. I liked her even more.

By the time Cindy arrived early for her shift, both the police car and the ambulance had gone. I didn't have time to fill her in on anything, for Johnny materialized beside me just as she entered. "C'mon with me, Cindy. We have a lot to do."

Following Johnny, Cindy looked at me in puzzlement and tilted her head in question, mouthing, "What's up?"

What could I say? She'd find out soon enough.

I headed home, but I knew Mike was not going to be there, so I'd be alone tonight. I was too exhausted to care. My mind continued to replay the scene of Richard taking his own life. When I arrived home, I took off my shoes and threw them in the trash. I picked up Sweet Pea, who had been waiting by the door, and carried her upstairs with me. I immediately took a shower in hopes the memories of what had happened would be washed away along with any residue that remained on me.

Afterwards I let Sweet Pea out to do her thing. I was as exhausted as I've ever been—both physically and emotionally. When we climbed the stairs again, I lifted Sweet Pea onto the bed and crawled in beside her. She cuddled next to me, and that was the last thing I remembered until she woke me up with kisses the next morning.

CHAPTER 17

T here was no fragrance of coffee brewing wafting to greet me, so Mike obviously wasn't home. Disappointed, I climbed out of bed and grabbed my robe. As I headed downstairs, I was surprised to see police cars next door. I exchanged my robe for my raincoat, slipped on my shoes, and went out to see what was happening. My neighbor, Ron, was standing there talking to the policemen, pointing my way. As I approached them, I called out, "Hey, Ron, what's going on?"

"I've called the police because there was a disturbance here last night. On my security system, I saw someone trying to get into your house. I just showed the tape to the officers here, and it's too blurry for them to make out who it might be. I'll have to adjust the camera," he added with regret.

One of the officers stepped forward and asked me, "Did you hear anything last night?"

"No, officer, I didn't hear a thing. I immediately went to bed after work and slept straight through the night."

"Do you always sleep so soundly, miss? If you do, you might need to step up your own security system," he added.

"Where's Mike?" asked Ron, interrupting us.

"He's away on business, Ron. Nothing to worry about."

"Humph," was all he said in return.

"Well, folks, I guess there's nothing more we can do here. Just remember to keep your doors and windows locked at all times. Let's go," he said to the other officer.

"Did *you* hear anything last night, Ron?" I asked when they were gone.

"Nooo. I was too tired and went to bed early as well. Actually, I slept better than I have for a while," he added with a guilty look. "But I always check my system every morning to be sure I haven't missed anything during the night. That's how I saw someone had been trying to get into your house."

"Good to know," I mumbled before turning back toward the house.

"Too bad we couldn't make out who it was," Ron called after me.

I was filled with unease. The person who came to mind was the man who had chased me at the mall, the same one I'd seen along the path at Lake Las Vegas. I'd speak to Brian about it today, and maybe he and Mike could track him down.

Sweet Pea was miffed at being left behind when I went to talk to Ron. I began to explain to her why I had, and she cocked her head and watched me intently while I talked.

I wondered what goes through a dog's mind during times like this. Do they hear what we say only as noise and tone so our words sound like waah, waah, waah? I smiled at the thought.

I called to Sweet Pea and let her out the back. As I did, I looked to the left of the door and saw that one of the plants close to the window was crushed, as if someone had stepped on it. We were so dry in Las Vegas that there was little chance of taking an impression of a footprint, but I'd make a mental note to show Brian and Mike the next time they were here. I waited for Sweet Pea to finish her daily duty and immediately locked the patio door as soon as we were back in the house.

I put on mediation music in hopes it would put me in a different frame of mind and soften the images of Richard's death, which were beginning to haunt me. I fed Sweet Pea, and as I began to fix my own breakfast, I could hear heavy footsteps coming up the front steps. Just to be on the safe side, I stealthily made my way to look through the peephole and saw Brian and Mike, looking exhausted. I opened the door to welcome them, and they practically fell in. "I've got coffee on. Let me get you guys a cup before you drop."

As they walked past me, I could smell cigarettes and booze. I knew neither smoked, but did they drink on the job? Not likely. "What have you two been up to?"

Both of them sat with their elbows rested on the table, and hands over their faces. "Oh my, that bad, is it?" I asked.

Brian looked up first, with worry in his eyes. "Did you know that Richard committed suicide at the lounge yesterday?"

My eyes filled, and I simply nodded, yes.

As I remained quiet, Mike looked up from the table and asked, "How come you didn't let us know?"

"You said you wouldn't be available," I defended myself. "Besides, I couldn't get to my phone because they blocked that area off."

Mike interrupted, "If Brian hadn't been on the scene with the police later ... oh, Rosie."

"What do you mean?" I asked, fear churning in the pit of my stomach.

Brian gave Mike a reproachful look, and in a softer, more encouraging voice, he asked, "Do you want to tell us about it?

At the look of surprise on my face, he continued, "I saw the print of a high heel on the carpet there and pretended to drop my camera on it and another one so they'd get smeared. Knowing how you tend to get yourself involved in things, I knew it was you who had been in there, because Mimi was wearing shoes with a different heel. She told us she was the only one besides Tony and Johnny who had been in that room."

"Oh, my god." My eyes continued to water, and several tears slid down my cheek, which made Brian and Mike uncomfortable. They held their ground and waited for me to begin my story. After I relayed every detail, they just looked at me in sorrow. They had seen things like that too many times themselves and knew the effect it was having on me.

"The shape you're in, I think you'd better call in sick today," ordered Brian.

"I can't do that; you know I can't."

"Give me one good reason you shouldn't follow my orders this time. Just once, that's all I ask," he snapped impatiently.

I said in a soft, even voice, using his proper name, "Brian, they kept quiet about what happened yesterday.

When I left last night, no one knew anything about it. I need to go back there today to find out how Mimi's going to handle this and other things going forward. If I call in sick, it leaves the door open to shut me out completely. You can't cut me loose now. And I can't leave Cindy there by herself."

Brian and Mike looked at each other. "She's got you there, Brian." Mike said.

Brian heaved a sigh. "I guess so," he admitted. "I'm too tired to argue anyway."

"Me too," said Mike. "Excuse me, you two, I'm going upstairs to bed. We're meeting this afternoon, right, Brian?" he asked as he got up from the table.

"Yeah. After you take Rosie to work, c'mon by."

I stood with Brian as he got ready to leave. He gave me a concerned look. "Listen, I need you to be careful. You have a way of attracting violence, and I want you safe."

He came closer and reached behind me, placing his hands at the small of my back, pulling me to him, and looking deep into my eyes. I was so surprised, expecting him to simply kiss me on the forehead as usual, that I forgot to untangle myself. We stood there with our arms wrapped around each other until I pulled away. Brian reached for me again until we were close enough for him to kiss my forehead, and then he walked to the door, where he turned and said "See you later, Rosie girl."

I felt conflicted. Yes, he was a handsome man any woman would be happy to have in her life, but, for many reasons, I was not ready for any relationship. I sighed. I had too much to do on my own.

CHAPTER 18

A s Mike drove me to work, he eyed me as I sat lost in thought. "Something's different with you, Rosie. Are you okay?"

"Yeah, I just have a lot on my mind. How about you?"

"Yup, the same." When Mike pulled into the lounge parking area, still two hours earlier than my usual shift, he searched my eyes before he lifted my chin up with closed fist and kissed me tenderly on one cheek and then the other. I shivered with pleasure, even though I thought he was just playing his part. I needed to be careful not to get too involved with either Brian or Mike, for it would be easy for them to break my heart.

Inside, Mimi herself greeted me. "I know how fast news travels around here, so you probably have heard by now what happened. You're aware that Richard committed suicide here yesterday afternoon, aren't you? I want us to be on the same page responding to anyone asking about it."

I swallowed hard. "Yes, I just heard about it, actually."

"So you know then. Good."

"How do you want me to handle it?" I asked with curiosity. "Are the police involved?"

"Yes. Everything's on the up and up with this. But I'm afraid this is just the beginning, because there're a lot of things going on here that need to be cleaned up if we're going to stay in business." She watched me for a few seconds. "The police are going to want to talk to you about your relationship with Richard because you worked for him at PUP. They should be here any minute. Just answer honestly."

My heart fell. I hated the thought of seeing the chief of police, much less having to discuss anything with him. However, I'd do everything I could to make our time together as short as possible.

"Here they are now." As she eyed my purse, which was still in my hand, she said, "I'm so sorry, I was in such a hurry to speak with you that I haven't given you time to put your purse away. Go do that, and I'll stall the policemen for a few minutes. Meet us in my office. You know where it is, right?"

I hesitated.

"It's just past the office the police have roped off."

I hurried along trying to gather my thoughts. I was happy to see that the chief of police hadn't come but instead had sent two of his men.

Mimi was sitting in the chair behind her desk when I got there, and I was glad to see she intended to sit in on the meeting. She pointed to the chair in front of her desk, inviting me to sit and face the two policemen, who were seated together on the small couch against the wall.

I was terrified that Sophia's death would be brought up; I wasn't sure what I'd say. I didn't want anyone to know I'd been involved with what happened then, especially since the actual day of her death did not jibe with the date people had been given. "So you knew Richard?" asked the first cop.

"Not really. I worked at PUP for just a couple of days before coming here. I saw him just one time. He asked me when I was scheduled to start here, and I told him. That's all."

"What do you know about his relationship with Sophia?" asked the other cop, studying me.

I wasn't about to reveal what Sophia had told me. "I know they worked together for several years. Why?"

"Just wondering if their relationship was more than business partners."

"What does that have to do with anything?" demanded Mimi. "Why bring her into this?"

"Just trying to get all the facts, ma'am," the first cop said.

"Now that Richard's dead, isn't it true that your family will get his percentage of the business?" the second cop asked Mimi. "That's part of the business agreement your father had with him, right?"

I saw that Mimi was getting annoyed, so I interrupted his line of questioning. "Can we please get back to any questions you want to ask me? I've got work to do."

"Just one more. Do you know anything about Richard's girlfriend, Sally?"

I was relieved that I could honestly say, "I didn't realize she was his girlfriend. As I said before, I saw Richard just that one time." As I said it, the vision I'd had of Richard at the time of Sally's death flashed before me, and I remembered the distraught look on his face. He must have really loved her. How sad.

"Do you need Rosalie for any more questions? You can see she didn't really know Richard and has nothing much to add," stated Mimi, emphatically. "I've a business to run here, so I'd appreciate it if you would button this up. I've already spent hours with you yesterday going over everything."

"Awright, go ahead. You can leave now," the second cop said to dismiss me.

As I rose, the first cop said, "Now I've got it—I knew I recognized you. You were Jeff's fiancée. Remember him, Charlie? The cop who was involved in all that mess a few years back?"

The second cop scrutinized me from head to toe. "Ah, yes. You're the one who gave us all that trouble, accusing us of lying and blaming him for the drug dealing that went on. You thought he was innocent, but you were too much in love to see the truth for what it was," he added smugly.

I could feel my face burn as my anger heated it. "And I remember you. You should be ashamed of yourselves, for I know you murdered Jeff, and don't you dare tell me you didn't. The truth will come out—it always does—and we'll see who has to face the truth then." Awkwardly, I made my way to the door.

"Thanks for your cooperation, Rosalie. It's time for you gentlemen to leave," commanded Mimi, as she rose from her chair and came around her desk to lead them to the door. "I'll walk you to the front."

God, I hate it when my buttons get pushed and I lose control. The confrontation with the police brought up all the old anger I felt, fair or not, toward any policeman. I really needed to rethink what I was getting involved in. Ever since I'd signed on to write a new column about what's going on in Las Vegas for *Women Living Well*, my whole world had turned upside down as I'd become immersed in so much violence and the seamier side of life. Is this how I wanted to live? Did what I was doing have any real value? How was it possible to stop all the terrible things going on? I'd seen more death within the past month than I had my entire life—first, there had been Melissa, then Sally, Sophia, Sam, David, and now Richard. All were gone.

And what about the little girls who'd been saved from the traffickers? Their trust that others would protect them was dead. I drew in long, ragged breaths and sent a prayer of love to the universe with the hope we'd all smarten up someday soon.

CHAPTER 19

O n her way back from escorting the police to the front door, Mimi stopped by the front desk. "We have time before our guests arrive. Why don't you take a break? I can see you're still upset, and a few minutes away from here to unwind will do you good. Go see Romano for a cup of tea or something."

"That'd be nice. Thank you, Mimi."

I wandered into Romano's kitchen, for I knew he deserved some answers about what had happened between us yesterday. He came out of the storage area, and when he saw me, he hesitated for a second and looked me over before he smiled broadly. He came toward me with concern written on his face. "How are you?"

"Oh, dear Romano, I'm so sorry. I know I upset you yesterday, but I didn't have a chance to sneak into the kitchen to see you before my shift ended. When I was getting ready to leave, I peeked in and saw you were swamped. What was that all about?"

"Each time I cook my chicken supreme, I'm always backed up with orders," he answered with a pleased smile. "Enough about that, my dear Rosebud, for I want to know what trouble you've gotten yourself into now. Here, take this cup of brewed tea and come sit with me. I think I've got a pretty good idea of what happened, but I want to hear it from you."

I shared my horrific experience of standing behind the louvered doors and watching Richard shoot himself. Romano's eyes were sad as he empathized with what I had gone through. "Oh, my darling girl, I thought it might be something like that. What are you going to do now?"

"Pretend nothing happened, just go along as usual."

"For you, nothing happening is *not* usual."

"It seems that way, doesn't it?" I asked, sadly. I looked at my watch and said, "Well, it's time for me to get back to work. I'll see you on my break if I may," I muttered listlessly.

"You bet," he answered before planting kisses on both my cheeks.

Mimi came out to sit with me at the front desk, and when we weren't dealing with guests, she said, "You don't have to talk about it if you don't want to, but I'd be interested in hearing your story about what happened to your fiancé, Jeff."

"Are you sure you have the time?" As she looked at me questioningly, I added, "No worries, I'll give you the short version."

Mimi was so different from the person I'd expected, especially coming from a family who was accused of being part of the New Jersey Mafia. She was strong, and there was no doubt she could be intimidating, for I'd heard her argue with Tony and even Johnny. She had demonstrated time and again she was their boss and was not about to let either one take over her position. But the thing I liked most about her was her brain—she had street smarts in addition to being business smart. It'd be interesting to see how she would handle things at the Purple Passion Lounge when all was said and done.

I intuitively knew I could trust her, so between guests coming in, I haltingly began, "Jeff was a cop. We met when he pulled me over for speeding after a night on the town with my girlfriends who were there for a visit. Our relationship grew, and after more than a year of exclusive dating, we made plans to marry. That, of course, never happened."

After another guest signed in, I picked up where I'd left off. "That was three years ago. He told me there was drug dealing going on in his department. Jeff was a pretty straight-up guy and didn't like what was happening. After he'd spoken up to the others and refused to be a part of it, he was in a car crash. Jeff was the only one in the car at the time, which was unusual to begin with. They usually patrolled in pairs, as partners. The cops' explanation was he'd fallen asleep at the wheel. I knew that couldn't have been what happened, because Jeff had a strict rule about never getting behind the wheel of a car unless he was in top shape to drive. He was obsessive about it."

When the next guest arrived, Mimi gave him directions to the bar area, and then I continued. "It was clear they'd made Jeff the fall guy for all that was going on in his department. I know they *murdered* him, it was obvious just from the way they acted so eagerly to say it was all Jeff's doing. When I tried to get the chief of police to listen to what I had to say, he instantly ordered that Jeff's body be cremated immediately. He got away with doing that because Jeff had no living relatives; because we weren't married yet, he didn't have to consider me."

Mimi was watching me intently. "What happened to the car Jeff was in?"

"Interesting you should ask," I responded with scorn. "It was immediately crushed and trashed 'because it was totaled,' our fair chief of police told me."

"That's quite a story, isn't it?" Mimi mused, looking distressed.

I could see my story had upset her. "Anything the matter?" I asked.

Even though she shook her head no, I felt uncomfortable and wasn't sure what she'd do with the information I'd shared with her.

Time passed quickly as a variety of clients came in, and Bambi once again came in to relieve me so I could take my break. She greeted me enthusiastically while she stuffed bills into the pocket of her robe. When she saw me watching her, she grinned. "Business is better than ever. After hearing about the shooting, I think most of the men coming here just like the excitement of being in a place where there was a murder. They even seem to get off on it. Weird, isn't it?"

I had to agree, for I'd seen that for myself. I headed to the kitchen to see Romano. I was so thankful to be able to sit there and take a break from the stress of Richard's death and my continued unease about working at the lounge.

When I stepped through Romano's doorway and heard the classical music he had playing, I relaxed even more and released some of the tension I'd felt when walking through the hallways and bar area. It was amazing that I couldn't feel any of negative energy there in his kitchen. Romano had been smart to set restrictions from the beginning to ensure that his kitchen domain was off-limits to anything going on outside his doors. I sighed, knowing I had changed that. It had worked for him up until I'd come into the picture and involved him in assisting me and helping the four little girls escape. It was a wonder he still wanted anything to do with me, yet, here he was, extending his hospitality to me once again.

Romano handed me a fabulous chicken salad sandwich to munch on when we sat down to talk. "Have you seen the little girls again?" he asked.

"Yes, I went to where they're staying. They were so cute and happy to see me again. And I'm afraid they've named me 'Loca' for good," I laughed.

He chuckled and repeated it. "Loca. It has a certain ring to it, don't you think?"

"Honestly, Romano, it's a pity they had to go through something like that, don't you agree?"

"Absolutely. What's going to happen to them?"

"The twins are already set to go back to Mexico to be with their parents. The other two are still here waiting to hear whether the agency has located their families. The oldest one, Isabella, calls me Mama and wants to live with me, if you can imagine that. You know I can't take that on, don't you?" I asked, defensively.

"Well, to be honest, I think you'd be a great mother."

"Thank you, but that's not in the cards right now. I have to tell you, though, the thing that bothers me the most is she is adamantly opposed to being returned to her parents, and I have a strong sense she isn't safe with her own family. It keeps coming to me that it wouldn't be a good thing for her to be returned to them, but I have no legal way to stop it."

"Well," responded Romano as he patted my hand, "the 'fat lady hasn't sung yet' about everything that's happening around here. We never know, do we, what can take place?"

"Not everything, for sure," I answered. "Since you've been here from the beginning of the change in this place, what can you tell me about the girls who used to work here?"

"What do you mean?" he asked with a furrowed brow.

"Did you get to know any of the girls who used to work here, and did you befriend them like you have Cindy and me?"

Romano became lost in thought. Then he turned to me and simply said, "One."

"What was her story? I'm trying to understand why girls are willing to do this. Yes, I know it's all about money, but still ..."

"You know there are many of us who keep our feelings inside. We keep a tight lid on our emotions, going along in life like a leaf in the wind instead of becoming the wind. But when a person decides to become the wind, there are times when everything becomes uncontrollable. That is what Susan was like. She'd been wound up tighter than a top, and when she finally let go of other people's expectations of her, it was as if she gave everyone the finger, saying. 'Fuck you all.' So, you see, it's not always about money. It can be about power and the freedom to become who you are."

I slowly nodded my head in agreement.

He smiled. "And that's what happened with me when I came out. By saying pretty much what Susan had, it gave me the power to be me. And that is worth more than any amount of money—at least to me."

I looked at Romano with new respect. It couldn't have been easy for him to announce to those closest to him that he was gay and would not be following the path they wanted or expected him to take. "Susan sounds like she could have been fun. What happened to her?"

Romano's face crunched up with disappointment. "I was away at the time, but I heard she'd gone too far. Nothing we didn't expect, for she was like a runaway freight train with no brakes. But I have to tell you, she was one of the most mesmerizing people I've ever met. You would have loved her. In an odd way, you remind me of her."

Seeing my surprise, he added, "When push comes to shove, you are not going to let anyone tell you what to do. You're going to always play your own music in life, no doubt about that," he added with a chuckle.

I looked at my watch and couldn't believe my time with Romano was up. In fact, I had only seconds to get back to the front in time. I literally ran.

CHAPTER 20

A little while later, Cindy arrived. She was still on the schedule Johnny had given her, coming in two hours early, although she wasn't working with him any longer to arrange the office for our new boss; Mimi had taken care of that herself. However, Cindy was now showing her a few things she needed to review.

Cindy liked Mimi almost as much as I did, so she wasn't that unhappy she hadn't been given David's job. She felt no rancor when Mimi took it. I was fascinated by watching them together, for they were quite a bit alike. They had self-assurance that was undeniable and made others look to them for leadership.

"Hey, Rosebud, how's it going?" asked Cindy as she hugged me in greeting.

"Okay. Did you ever meet Susan, one of the girls who used to work here?" I asked.

"No. Why?"

"Just curious to know what exactly happened to her."

"Ask Romano. Maybe he'll know."

"All he said is she'd gone too far. I had a sense that maybe knowing what'd happened to her might be tied to our own investigation."

Cindy reached for me, and gave me another hug, whispering, "Brian told me what happened yesterday. I'm so sorry."

Her loving concern caused uninvited tears to come to my eyes. I brushed them away and asked, "How many deaths have you witnessed?"

"Two, and that's enough as far as I'm concerned. But in this line of work, you never know," she said with a grim expression. To change the subject, she asked, "Isn't Mimi a hoot? I really like her, don't you?"

I nodded yes. As we stood together looking out the one-way window, my heart lifted as we watched both Brian and Mike approach the front door. They certainly were a handsome pair. I could feel Cindy by my side, straightening the dress she was wearing, for she wanted to be at her best to greet them, particularly Mike.

It was obvious both men were tired, and it showed as they dutifully greeted us with perfunctory hugs and kisses. "What's going on?" I asked.

They looked at each other questioning whether this was the place to talk. Then Brian whispered, "David Masterly's autopsy report came back, and you're not going to believe this—he had stage 4 cancer and only a few weeks to live, according to the coroner. And here's the biggest news—he wasn't murdered; he committed suicide. We even recovered the gun he used from the lake."

"That doesn't make sense," I exclaimed in a loud whisper. "What was he doing out at Lake Las Vegas?"

"One of the girls we interviewed told us he'd found out you were staying there and wanted to warn you," Brian responded.

"You've got to be kidding. He didn't even know my name, for God's sake. Why would he even care what happened to *me*? And how did he know I was out there to begin with? "

"Hold on, Rosie, and we'll explain," said Brian. "David mumbled something to this girl that he didn't want another murder on his conscience." Then he added, "We'll get to the bottom of this."

"Let's discuss this further at home, shall we?" asked Mike, looking at us.

It felt so natural to hear him say that—as if our "going home" together were becoming a common practice. I was tired, distraught, and sick of everything going on around me. I pressed my hands to my eyes and took a deep breath. "I'll get my purse and be right back."

They silently watched me leave. As I passed by the kitchen, I blew Romano a kiss and continued on. When I approached the employee lounge, I heard someone crying. I opened the door to find Shirley, the newest young recruit to the dance troupe, sitting at the table and talking on the phone with tears streaming down her face. "I'm not going to give up this job. We need the money so we can get married …"

I tiptoed around her and headed to my locker. I heard Shirley sniff and then say, "No, I don't want to elope, I want a regular marriage and a honeymoon, just like everyone else."

As I grabbed my purse, closed my locker, and turned to leave, Shirley raised her voice, snapping, "You can't tell me what to do. I'm free to do what I want."

I gave her a tender pat on her head and mouthed, "Good luck." as I moved past her.

She smiled at me and nodded.

Mike, Cindy, and Brian were huddled together whispering. They turned as one when they heard me come up, and each wore the guilty expression we all have when we're caught talking about someone who's within earshot. "What have you all been talking about?" I demanded.

"Let's just go home for now, Rosie," said Mike.

I was too tired to pursue anything. Cindy approached me and hugged me good night, whispering, "You're in good hands. See you tomorrow."

I was glad to be home and hugged Sweet Pea to me closer than usual. She looked at me with worry but let me hold her tight. It seemed as if I were an octopus, with all my tentacles twisted together and holding onto different aspects of all the deaths that had taken place. My mind was too fried to make sense of it all. I told Mike, "I have to go to bed. I can't think straight, but I'll talk to you in the morning."

He looked at me with concern, "I think that's a good idea, and don't worry about a thing. I'll be here all night."

I was hoping that sleeping would make things more clear, as often happens when I'm in that state where things are allowed to unravel on their own.

Instead, I tossed and turned, and all the events remained tangled. I got up with a sense of urgency about working on the written codes I'd kept hidden from Brian in the beginning of the investigation—those codes that Melissa had left me, and which I now believed had caused Sally's death. I removed them from my safe place in the closet, went downstairs, and made a photocopy so I wouldn't ruin the original.

Mike wasn't up yet, which surprised me until I looked at the clock and saw it was only 4:30 a.m. Sweet Pea hadn't even followed me downstairs, for I'm sure she wasn't about to miss any of her early-morning sleep—unless it was for Mike. She was beginning to get attached to him and used to his being there, and she'd be sorry when he left. To be honest, it would be hard for both of us to adjust.

I searched the anagrams of the coded pages, unsure whether I'd be able to decipher them. It was obvious each line named a person and a product, and it was also easy to spot "B.B." It became even more interesting when I noticed it looked as though he was owned credit or money, while the other lines looked like debits or money due. I now felt strongly David Masterly wasn't B.B. and knew we'd have to move past thinking he was, and begin to look at someone else. One of the words in several lines that threw me was "robbery bath." Another was "thy anon," which I was pretty sure stood for Anthony—meaning Tony. "Noh" was also used, which it was easy to figure out stood for John or Johnny. Also there was "heartb," an identity that would be interesting to figure out.

I heard Mike coming down the stairs and then in the kitchen, obviously starting the coffee. I could also hear Sweet Pea, her nails sounding like tap dancing on the floor. The odor of coffee brewing wafting up pulled me into the kitchen. "Good morning, Mike."

He jumped, for I'd startled him. "My god, woman, you almost gave me a heart attack."

"Sorry," I said as I tried to hold back a chuckle. "I got up to do some research on those coded pages Melissa left me, but I found nothing we hadn't expected. According to Brian, we can't use it for evidence, just information for us to pursue, right?"

"Pretty much," he responded. "We can't prove where the pages came from, so they can't be used as evidence."

"I dunno, Mike. I've a feeling they're holding a clue. Oh, well, maybe not."

"Ready for a cup of coffee?" asked Mike, interrupting my thoughts.

"Sure thing. I think it'd be a good idea to meet and discuss where we are on the murders of Melissa and Sally. What do you think?"

"Sure," he answered.

"Shall we call in Brian?" I asked, knowing he wouldn't want to be left out.

"Yeah, that'd be good. I'll give him a call after breakfast."

"Sounds good." I was keen to settle those deaths once and for all. I was disgruntled by the fear they'd become cold cases.

CHAPTER 21

When Brian arrived, he hurried in and barely missed Sweet Pea, who was instantly at
his feet, nearly tripping him. He bent down, swung her
up into his arms, and rushed into the kitchen. Mike and
I were already seated at the table, jotting down notes,
when he skidded to a complete stop before us. "Guess
what?"

Mike and I were surprised to see him so excited. "What
now?" I asked.

"My friend from the police department called to tell me
they've arrested two teenagers for Sam's murder."

"You're kidding. You mean his death had nothing to
do with all the others tied to PUP or the Purple Passion
Lounge?"

"That's exactly what I'm saying. Can you believe it? These two kids are only 15 years old. They said it was a botched robbery."

"I'd certainly say so, since Sam's wallet was found next to him with all his money still in it," I confirmed.

"What did they say happened?" Mike asked, curious.

"One of the kids said Sam recognized him, so they had no choice but 'to do him in.' That's a quote, by the way. What he said next is even more bizarre. He said they had no choice because if their parents found out they were involved in a robbery, they'd be in real trouble for sure."

"What the hell?" Mike exclaimed. "Kids today watch too much television where every bit of trouble seems to blow over in the quick hour it takes for the show to end. They just don't get it. They never see the fallout of their actions or want to take responsibility for their own actions," he ended in disgust.

Obviously, this new information had hit a nerve with Mike. There had to be a story behind it, and I wondered what it was. I didn't ask, though, for I knew it must be personal. It was clear he was not about to share it with us, since he immediately rose from his chair and began to pace slowly around the room, deep in thought. I looked at Brian, who lifted his shoulders and shook his head to indicate we'd better leave Mike alone with his thoughts.

Then Mike returned to the table and asked, "Anyone for more coffee?"

Brian and I declined, and I asked Brian, "So how are we going to find the killer or killers of Melissa and Sally?"

Brian looked discouraged. "It's got to be someone tied into the Purple Passion Lounge, don't we all agree?"

Mike and I nodded. "However, the district attorney won't allow anyone to make a move until there's more evidence, so for now, we just keep doing what we've been doing. That's all we can do."

"I suppose," I said, disappointed.

"Are you still scheduled to work at the lounge seven days a week?" asked Brian.

"Actually, I've been told I can take Mondays off. Cindy has Tuesdays off."

"That's good. So tomorrow, you're off. Maybe you can…"

"Just a minute, Cowboy." I interrupted. "Don't go any further. I have a lot to do."

"What I was going to say before you *rudely* interrupted me is maybe you could relax and unwind for a change."

Mike, watching us, said, "You two," and shook his head.

I was a little chagrinned but not about to let what Brian said take over. "I'm sorry. I guess I'm just out of sorts."

"No worries," he conceded. "We're all on edge because we seem to be stuck in our investigation. We need to interview the older lady at Sally's complex again to see if she can recall anything more than she did last time. She's had time to reflect on it and might have something new to tell us."

"I can do that, if you want," I immediately spoke up. "Woman to woman, you know," I added, trying to be helpful.

"I thought you wanted time to relax, but hey, if you want to do that interview, go for it," he responded, happy to have me partnering with them on that.

"Just send me the info so I can call her, please."

"Sure. Then Mike, maybe you can follow up with Melissa's roommate. I heard she's back in town for some event."

"Sounds good. Do you know where she's staying?"

"At the Bellagio, I'm pretty sure."

As soon as Brian mentioned the Bellagio, my mind wandered back to the time I'd met Sally there. She had been desperate to see whether I had something she believed Melissa had taken. I hadn't known at the time she wasn't interested in the money that Melissa had left with me but the codes that were hidden in the package. Now both girls were dead. And who had followed Sally to our meeting?

I closed my eyes and in my mind went back again to that time. The man's hair had an odd wave in it, and I now knew without a doubt it had been Johnny. Back then, I had yet to meet him. Yes, indeed, it was Johnny who had hustled Sally out of there. "What about Johnny, Brian? What's going on with him?"

"He certainly has been well counseled. He and Tony haven't taken one step out of line and still are pretending they're perfectly law-abiding businessmen. We haven't been able to get a lousy thing on either of them yet—or at least not enough to pull them in."

"That's too bad," I said with resignation.

"We'll get them, not to worry," responded Mike with determination.

"Well, I guess that's it. I'm out of here then," announced Brian. "See you all later."

I headed into my office to make a list of the things I needed to get done—things I'd fallen behind on because of all my sleuthing. Fortunately, I had a folder full of articles I had saved for times like this when I got behind writing for the magazine.

I passed my parents' gold antique mirror and glanced at myself. Ohh, my—it was time to bite the bullet and get my hair cut and done by the hairdresser that Louie, my fashion designer, had suggested. God bless him for all of his clothing advice and help. Before I could change my mind, I grabbed the number I had written down in my address book and dialed. I was surprised to get an appointment right away, but the girl explained, "You're one of the lucky ones. There usually is a 30-day wait because he is in such demand, but he just had a cancellation for tomorrow morning, and I'm giving it to you."

Working at the lounge that night was easy. Time slipped along without any surprises or upheavals—one of those periods that just seem to flow without any hiccups. Before I realized it, it was time to head home. It felt like a magical night because I knew I didn't have to return to the lounge the next day. Even Cindy noticed how peaceful I seemed and commented, "You sure look relaxed. Everything go okay?"

"Yup," I answered dreamily. "Nothing much happening for a change. It kinda feels funny, though," I said with a chuckle, "to have things so quiet."

"Let's hope it stays that way for a while at least," Cindy added with a smile.

"From your lips to God's ears," I proclaimed.

By the time I arrived home, I was grateful not to have to meet with anyone to discuss the investigation. There was nothing to interfere with my having a fabulous glass of wine to sip while I listened to romantic music. Mike was supposed to work late with Brian—both were tailing different people—so the place was all mine. All mine and Sweet Pea's, of course.

I let Sweet Pea out and watched her from the patio doorway as she did her thing and then scurried back inside. After I locked the door and pulled the shutters closed, I poured a glass of Pinot, wandered into the living room, and plopped down in the comfy chair by the fireplace. I tuned into an internet music station, and I found music by Eva Cassidy. What a voice she had.

When I was about to relax and sink deeper in the chair, my phone rang. It was late and past most people's bedtime, so I simply chose to ignore it, as it probably was just another sales call. Instead, I pushed back into the chair and leaned my head back. I set my wine down and closed my eyes, and became caught up in the music. That was the last thing I remembered until I heard Sweet Pea growling.

CHAPTER 22

I was disoriented and unsure of why Sweet Pea was on notice. She must have heard something; she was now up on all fours and alert, facing the front door. We both listened for any more sounds. Nothing. Since all was quiet for the moment, I settled back into my chair, in no rush to come fully awake. Then we both heard it again—a soft tap, tap, tap. I got up and headed to the front door, trying to be silent as I moved. I looked through the peephole and didn't see anything, so I whispered, "Who's there?"

A scared little voice called out, "Mama? It's me, Isabella."

I quickly opened the door and was dumbfounded to see her standing there. "What are you doing here? How did you get here?" I asked as I pulled her inside.

She looked at me sorrowfully. I knew she expected me to be happy to see her rather than bark questions at her.

"Come here," I said, opening my arms to welcome her. She ran into them and hugged me close around the waist.

"I want to be with you," she said.

"You know that's not possible, don't you?" I asked in a tender but stern voice.

Isabella looked up at me and nodded her head up and down. "I know," she sighed.

I gently pushed her away and looked at what she was wearing. She was a mess—her clothes were dirty and wrinkled. "Here's what we're going to do. I'm going to start running a tub for you and put your clothes in the laundry. I'll call Maria and let her know you are safe with me and will be spending the night here, okay?"

Isabella enthusiastically bobbed her head in agreement and jumped up and down with excitement. I'd have to enforce the idea that this wasn't a reward for disobeying the rules; this had to be the one and only exception.

I hurriedly called Maria, who answered on the second ring. She was relieved to hear my voice. "I'm not surprised she's with you. You're all she talks about."

"How did she get here, Maria? I thought she was safe with you," I said accusingly.

"I know, I thought so too. When I asked Mariana, she told me Isabella had gone into my office when I wasn't looking and copied your address. She said Isabella was determined to find you. She said goodbye to her and simply took off. I don't know much more than that …"

"Let's get to the bottom of this so it won't happen again. Let me put her on the phone so she can explain."

"Yes, please, since I'm the one in trouble now. I'll have to answer to the agency."

"Isabella," I called to her. "I want you to talk to Maria and tell her just how you got here."

With excitement, she grabbed the phone. I heard some of the pride in her voice as she spoke in a flurry of Spanish. There was silence as she listened to Maria, and then she hung her head. "Here," she said in a quiet voice as she handed me the phone, obviously upset. "Maria wants to speak to you."

Maria was beside herself. "You are not going to believe this. Isabella said she intended to simply walk to your house. She thought all she had to do was show someone your address she'd written down, and they'd show her the way to you."

I could hear the panic in her voice as she continued, "She was very lucky. The first person she asked was a girl she met at the fast-food place right around the corner. Fortunately, she was Mexican and able to understand her. Isabella climbed into a car with her and some of her other girlfriends, who must have taken pity on her when she said she was to meet her mama. Oh, my god, Rosalie, she has no idea what could have happened."

Maria trailed off, and we both were silent for a moment as we realized that Isabella knew all too well what could happen. "All right, Maria, I'll speak to her. We'll work together to make sure this doesn't happen again. Meantime, any word on her family?"

"I'm not supposed to tell you this, but they've located her family in Mexico. They don't want her back. We're still tracking down some of her other relatives who may be here in the States. We'll have to wait and see what happens."

I felt the horror of how it would feel for Isabella to discover her own family didn't want her back, even if she proclaimed she didn't want to be returned to them. "Maria, I think a little R&R for our little girl is what she needs right now, don't you? I have tomorrow off, so I'd like to spend some of the day with Isabella and return her to you later, if that's okay. Does that work for you?"

"It's not up to me, but I think I can make that happen with the agency. They have your telephone number, don't they, if they need to speak with you directly?"

"Yes, they do. Thanks so much, Maria, and don't worry. She's safe now."

I hung up and felt a pang in my heart, for no one likes to be rejected in any way, particularly by family. Well, I'd do my best to make the next day special for Isabella— but only if she promised she'd never do anything like this again.

The bubbles rose high in the tub, hiding Isabella's petite body, allowing just her milky brown face and wide grin to show. Her dark eyes sparkled, and her freshly shampooed hair glistened. She was beautiful. There was no denying it.

I looked at her and shivered with the knowledge she'd have brought a high price from anyone seeking to purchase her. I became even more determined to do what I could to stop the human trafficking of young girls, which had become so widespread today.

After her bath, I put her into one of my nightgowns, which hung from her body and dragged on the floor. I tucked her into bed in the second guest room and sat with her for a few minutes until her eyes closed in sleep. I tiptoed out of the room and left the door ajar so there'd be enough light to guide her way to the bathroom, where a nightlight glowed. I headed into my own bedroom to ready myself for bed. After changing out of my clothes, brushing my teeth, and cleansing my face, I walked back into my room and turned off the light. As I slipped into bed, I was surprised to discover Isabella under the covers with Sweet Pea curled up next to her.

"Ahh, so this is how it's going to be then—two against one. Okay, you win for tonight. Sweet dreams, my darling girls." Just Sweet Pea was awake enough to look at me, happy and smiling her special smile.

In the wee hours of the morning, I awakened and rolled over to see two dark eyes staring at me. I reached over, smoothed Isabella's hair, and smiled at her. I looked at the clock and realized she'd probably heard Mike come in. "It's not time to get up yet. Just roll over and go back to sleep."

She looked at me with questions in her eyes. "It's okay. You just heard Mike come in. Remember him? He helped save us. He's going to bed now, but we'll see him in the morning, okay?"

She nodded. "Okay."

I slept like a log and woke up with the smell of coffee calling me. I looked at the clock and realized I was usually up long before this. I rolled over to find I was alone in my bed—Sweet Pea was no longer there, and neither was Isabella. I jumped out of bed, grabbed my robe, and headed downstairs. As I approached the kitchen, I heard Isabella's laughter and then Mike's. My heart lifted with joy.

As I entered the kitchen, Mike called out, "Hey, sleepyhead, good morning."

After Isabella figured out the term "sleepyhead," she began to giggle. "Loca sleepyhead."

Out of the mouths of babes, I thought. They have a way of bringing everything right down to the basics. I smiled and tugged her hair as I passed by her. "Good morning, Mike. You sure were late coming home last night. Anything interesting happen?"

"Naw, everyone seems to be watching their step and not making any waves, so for now, it's still the same."

"Well, obviously, you can see that Isabella spent the night here. We're going to spend part of the day together before I return her to Maria later on. We had a talk about the dangers of just taking off like she did. She promises to stay with Maria and not run away again; right, Isabella?"

Isabella looked down at the plate set before her. She simply nodded in agreement, as she knew she had no choice.

Mike confirmed her good sense by adding, "Good girl. That's the smart thing to do."

At his praise, she looked up and searched his face, wondering if he'd meant what he'd said. As she studied him and found no reason not to believe other than what he'd said, she smiled. Whether Mike knew it or not, he had just made a friend for life.

CHAPTER 23

I removed Isabella's clothes from the dryer and smoothed them out before handing them to her to put on. She was so excited it was catching. We laughed and twirled around each other as if we both were young girls with no worries. I gathered her in my arms and hugged her tight. "Okay, kiddo, let's get ready for our big day at Richard's."

Isabella smiled and seemed to release any trepidation about what was coming next. "Okay," is all she said, bouncing up and down on her toes.

I drove to Richard's salon, hoping one of the other beauticians would be able to fit Isabella into their busy schedule while I was there. As we walked through the door, we found welcoming smiles greeted us as well as interest in Isabella. I was pleased beyond belief when it turned out that Yvonne was going to have time to give

171

Isabella a haircut. They were so cute together, laughing and speaking Spanish. I felt a pang of jealousy, for I knew only a few words of Spanish. That would have to change, I thought.

Richard was something else again. Bless Louie, dear Louie, for recommending him to me as someone who might be able to control my hair and actually do something with it. Richard had tufted purple hair and a wide smile that covered his entire lower face while his large brown eyes danced with delight and several gold earrings in each ear drew your attention to them. He flitted around me, lifting up my hair and letting it drop while shaking his head in dismay. "Tsk, tsk, darling girl, what have we here?"

My crooked smile should have been a warning to anyone who caught my expression as it changed from apprehension to annoyance, but Richard didn't acknowledge my discomfort. "No worries. When I finish with you, all will be just right."

"Just what are you going to do with my hair?" I asked, nervously.

"Not to worry. It's going to be beautiful," he stated as he reached for his scissors.

"Aren't you going to wash my hair first?"

"That's the mistake all amateurs make. You want to let nature show you how the hair falls, which doesn't happen when it's wet and not natural."

"You're not going to make it too short, are you?"

"I'm going to turn your chair around so you can't watch me do my magic," he stated, leaving me no choice as he swiveled me away from the mirror.

I sat helpless, close to tears. My hair was such an important part of my personality, and truth be told, I didn't want to look like everyone else. However, I decided to let go of my concern about what Richard was doing, and as I did, I smelled roses—a sign my grandmother was near. I could sense her delight that someone other than she was tackling my hair. Too many times in the past, she had been the one to suffer my dislike of having anyone fussing over my hair. Those memories made me smile.

Two hours later, Isabella and I left the salon, both wearing smiles and feeling very beautiful. "It's time for lunch," I said. "Shall we go to Nordstrom's for a bite to eat and a little shopping?"

She looked up at me with uncertainty. "Really?"

"Yes, really," I said, hugging her close.

Very shyly, she looked at me and said, "Your hair different. Very beautiful."

I glowed with her compliment. It was the same hair style I usually wore, but it was nicely trimmed and cut so my hair flowed—but with more style. I was pleased and would have to make sure to thank Louie for suggesting Richard.

"And you too, my beautiful Isabella."

When we entered Nordstrom's, I got goose bumps. I looked around nervously, feeling uneasy. As I searched the store, I thought I saw the same man who had followed me at Lake Las Vegas and into the mall. Pulling Isabella along with me, I hurriedly marched over and stopped in front of him. When he saw me approach, he quickly turned his back and pretended to be interested in women's dresses.

"Just what is it you want?" I demanded.

"What do you mean, lady? I'm just shopping here."

"Puhleeze. Stop the shit and tell me what it is you want of me," I demanded in a harsh whisper, while covering Isabella's ears with my hands.

He hadn't expected me to approach him, and he was embarrassed to be caught and confronted by me. "If you don't tell me right now, I'll scream for the security guard," I threatened.

"Calm down, lady, it's okay. Tony just wants to make sure you're all right. I'm just following orders to make sure you're safe, that's all."

"So why didn't *he* tell me that?" I demanded. "Why all the secrecy?"

"You'll have to ask to him. I'm just following orders."

"Well, just leave us alone. If I see you around us again, I'll call for security, do you understand?"

"Okay, okay, just stay calm. I'll go," he promised.

"I'll take care of this with Tony myself, understood?" I said.

At that, he left, I stood there wondering why Tony would be interested in protecting me. From whom? My attention was quickly diverted when Isabella ran to a stuffed teddy bear that wore a big heart on his chest. "Oh, Mama, he's so pretty."

"Would you like to keep him for yourself?" I asked. As she nodded, I added, "Then you'll need to pick out a toy for Mariana too." I knew the twins were on their way back to their parents, and it was only Isabella and Mariana now with Maria.

"Yes, Mama." It was fascinating to watch her go from one stuffed animal to the next, carefully picking up each one and holding it to see which one felt the best. After testing nearly all of them, she handed me a stuffed rabbit that was darling.

"Good girl, Isabella. You picked the best one for her." Isabella just smiled and clung tight to the bear in her arms.

"How about we look at some shorts and tops for you and Mariana?"

Isabella just stared at me as if she hadn't understood what I'd said. "C'mon, follow me," I said as I headed toward the children's department. When we got there, I became enthralled by all the choices, for the clothes were stylish and so much more so than what was available when I was a child. It was going to be hard for me to choose, but I needn't have worried, because Isabella made it very clear she was going to be the one to pick out her clothes; she didn't need any help from me. She ran right up to a mannequin wearing a pretty outfit about her size. She turned and smiled at me. "Mine," she said, which was enough for me to agree.

The sales clerk who waited on us laughed at Isabella's scurrying around and pulling at all the clothes. We ended up with two outfits, underwear, and a pair of pajamas each for Isabella and Mariana. Isabella was a girl who knew what she wanted, and she wasn't afraid to express it. I had to smile when she relented and let me pick out an outfit for Mariana.

Our lunch at Nordstrom's café was an organic pizza, soda, and brownies for dessert—none of which was particularly healthy but tasted wonderful. I decided that it was best not to wait any longer to return Isabella to Maria so that she could get resettled. That way, I'd be able to see whether I could interview the older lady who lived in Sally's complex.

"It's time to return you to Maria," I said in a firm but gentle voice.

Isabella just stared at me in defiance. "I mean it, Isabella. We've had a lovely time together, but it's time for you to share the treats with Mariana so she can have a little furry friend too."

Slowly, she nodded her head in agreement. "All right, let's go," I said and we headed to the valet area to get my car. As we drove back to Maria's house, I felt a pang of regret that I was returning her a bit early, but I needed to get back to do my part in discovering who killed Melissa and Sally. I also had to make it clear to Isabella that our retreat today was not a reward for running away and coming to me. My thoughts were reeling as I turned to her. "Isabella, I need to know you are safe. Do you understand me?"

When she nodded, I continued, "So I need to know you are with Maria and not out alone at night with no protection. I don't want you to run away or come to my house again. You were lucky to find me at home, because sometimes I'm not there. You need to remember that any time a girl like you is by herself, with no one else around, day or night, you are in danger. Do you understand what I'm saying?" I asked.

Slowly, Isabella nodded. "So never do that again, do you hear me? Never again," I stated firmly. "I have to trust you to do what I say. Do you understand me?"

Isabella looked at me with sorrow. "Yes, Mama, I understand."

"Good," I said as I reached over and patted her leg tenderly. "Good."

When we got back to Maria's, Mariana was the first to greet us by running out the front door and racing to Isabella before we'd even gotten out of the car. She began speaking to Isabella in rapid Spanish, obviously upset by being left behind, but Isabella distracted her with the shopping bags.

Curious now, Mariana poked at one of the bags Isabella pushed toward her. As she opened the bag with the stuffed rabbit, she squealed with delight, and Isabella and I looked at each other and smiled at her pleasure. Maria joined us and exclaimed over everything the girls pulled out of their bags. It was a happy time, and I knew this was something the girls would remember forever.

Maria called me aside and said, "The agency allowed you to take Isabella this time, but they want to make sure you know this is just a one-time thing. We don't encourage anyone getting closely involved with any of the girls because it makes it that much harder for everyone. You understand, don't you?"

"Of course, I understand completely. I wouldn't want to be responsible for upsetting Isabella no matter what happens. Thank you, Maria, for allowing us this special time together. I will always remember your kindness."

I called both girls over and gave them a group hug. I pulled Isabella's arms from around my waist so I could look her in the eyes. "No matter what happens, I know you'll do the right thing, the thing that is best for you. I love you and I always will. I can't be your mama, but know that if I ever have a little girl, I hope she's just like you—strong, smart, and beautiful."

Isabella bit her lower lip, determined not to cry, while I, on the other hand, fought back tears. We hugged one last time, and I turned away in a hurry, making my way to my car and my other life.

CHAPTER 24

Before I'd left home with Isabella, I'd written down the telephone number of the neighbor in Sally's development, which Brian had forwarded to me. Now I dialed it on the car's Bluetooth. Fortunately, she answered right away. "Hello?"

"Hello. My name is Rosalie Bennett. I'm writing a story on your neighbor Sally's murder, and I was wondering whether you'd be kind enough to let me interview you. Would you answer a few questions for me?"

I could hear the excitement in her voice as she asked, "Is it going to be on TV or the radio? I prefer television because more people watch television than listen to the radio, don't you agree?"

Ah ha, I thought. She's older and probably a little lonely, needing some attention, so I'd work with that. "Well, I'm writing an article about the murder in a top magazine, which I'm not supposed to reveal just yet. Why don't we see how the interview goes? If there is some new information about the case, I'll call in the photographer to take some additional photos. How does that sound?"

"Well, I guess that's okay."

"When are you available to meet? Can you meet now?" I urged.

"Oh my, you sure are in a hurry, but I guess it doesn't matter to me. One day wanders into the next, and they're all the same anyway. Okay, c'mon over now if you like. Do you know which apartment is mine?"

"Yes, I do. And thanks so much for meeting with me on such short notice. I have a deadline for the story, so this works out just fine. See you soon."

As I headed her way, I realized that if she had some new information for us, this could be her great moment. If so, I wanted to make sure I treated her in the proper manner. I didn't want to promise her anything I couldn't deliver, because it would be up to Brian to determine how to handle anything I learned. When I reached Sally's neighbor's door, I rang the bell and shook her hand, reintroducing myself. "Mrs. Wellborn, I'm Rosalie Bennett. Thank you for seeing me."

She was a small lady with light blue eyes that blended with her blue-gray hair, something I hadn't seen in years— not since some of my grandmother's clients used to tint their hair that shade. Back then, hair dyed that way used to intrigue me because it was so very different from my grandmother's hair, which remained dark until she died. Mrs. Wellborn wore a pleasant smile and invited me in. "C'mon in, dear. I've put some tea on for us."

"Oh, how nice," I responded sincerely. A cup of tea would hit the spot.

"Here, dear, you sit right here, and I'll be back with the tea. Do you take sugar?"

"Just one lump, please," I replied, intuitively knowing she still used sugar cubes.

When she returned, she had not only my tea but also a plate of store-bought tea crackers, a type of cookie I hadn't seen in ages. I politely took one along with my cup of tea. I could sense Mrs. Wellborn gearing up for having me as her captive audience, so I sat back and resigned myself to the idea I was going to be there for a while—and she did not fail me. It was tough to keep her on track of exactly why I was there for an interview. Finally, I said, "Mrs. Wellborn, I need to leave soon, so it's important we discuss Sally's case. Another day we can finish up the other things you want to discuss, all right?"

"Do you mean it? Will you really come back?"

I'd put myself into a corner, but I would stick to what I'd said. "I promise I will."

"Okay, dear, what exactly do you want to know?"

"The night that Sally was killed, you told the police you didn't see anything, but you thought you heard skirmishes. Is that right?"

"Well, partly. I was talking to the handsome reporter about the case. Do you know which one I mean, the one on Channel 5?"

I nodded my head and smiled to myself. Yes, all the ladies seemed to like Brian.

"Well, I was about to tell him something that I thought was odd at the time, but the police came over to where we were talking outside and started pushing him away from me. They ordered me to go into my apartment and stop talking to the press. I didn't like the way they treated the reporter or me, so I decided that was it—the police weren't going to get anything out of me."

"Did the police ask to speak to you?

"Yes, the pushy one did, but I told him I had nothing to say. And that was it. They probably thought I was just some old foolish lady anyhow," she said in a voice that implied she'd heard that before.

"Sometimes the old foolish ladies of the world are the smart ones, aren't they?" I commented. "What were you going to tell the reporter, if you don't mind my asking?"

She stared long and hard at me evaluating whether she should tell me and finally said, "I can tell you're okay." She leaned back and closed her eyes to bring the memory to the forefront. She continued in a soft voice, "I knew Sally was upset. If she saw me standing at my window, she usually waved and blew me a kiss. That night she never even looked up, only rushed to the front door of the apartment building. At first, I simply thought she must've had a bad day—nothing more than that."

She lowered her voice and explained "Our apartment building is a bit older, and the floors and walls aren't the thickest. Since she lived below me, I could sometimes hear bits and pieces, you know." She looked at me expressively. "I tried to let her have her privacy as much as I could. You understand, don't you?"

I nodded my head and said, "Of course I do. It's not always easy though, is it?" I asked, knowing full well she took advantage of the situation.

She nodded in agreement while trying to gather her thoughts. "Anyway, that night I heard the front door open and close several times, one right after another, which was somewhat unusual, although it can happen. About an hour after Sally came home, I thought I heard some arguing going on, but in loud whispers. Then I heard Sally call out for her mother, which was very strange because I know for a fact her mother died years ago."

She sat straight up in her chair fully satisfied. "That's it. That's what I was going to tell that handsome reporter."

"What exactly did she say?" I asked, trying to fill in what she meant.

"She called out, 'Mama.'"

I was filled with excitement; Sally most likely was calling Bertha by her nickname—Mama. "Did you hear the front door open or close after that?"

"No, but I believe I heard running and the back door of the apartment slam shut, but it's far enough away that I couldn't be sure."

I was excited by this information, and I began to rise from my chair. "Well, you certainly have been a big help, Mrs. Wellborn, and I appreciate your time. Why don't you stay seated right where you are while I take a picture of you with my phone? I'll send it in to our photographer, and we'll see whether he'll be able to use this one or he'll need to come out here in person."

I suddenly felt light-headed and had to sit down again. I had a vision of Sally yelling "Mama" at Bertha, who was across the room from her, but Bertha wasn't alone. I saw a shadowy larger figure standing over Sally, but I couldn't make out who it was. So Mama was involved with these murders but wasn't the killer?

"Are you okay?" asked Mrs. Wellborn, watching me with concern.

"Yes, just a little light-headed, but I'm fine, really I am," I responded with a forced smile.

After realizing just how photogenic Mrs. Wellborn was, I ended up taking several pictures in case we actually were going to use them for any media or report. She was pleased and gave me a hug before I left. "Remember, you promised you'd return."

I knew she wouldn't let me forget.

CHAPTER 25

When I got home, I was surprised to see Mike wearing a worried expression. "I tried calling you several times and couldn't reach you."

I blushed with embarrassment. "I'm so sorry. I put my phone on silent while I was interviewing Sally's neighbor, and I must have forgotten to turn it back on. Why? What's up?"

"Mama's missing. Apparently, she has been gone for a few days now, and no one knows where she is. From now on, you can't be out of my sight for a minute, since Mama threatened to get even with you for all the mess you created for her. That means you absolutely can't run off on your own for anything. So wherever you are, you have to have me or Brian close by, understood?"

"Wow, Mama's missing, is she? That's certainly not great news." I thought about my situation for a moment and added, "I'll be safe at work with everyone around, so that's good. And having my next-door neighbor, Ken, as our surveillance expert able to record anything going on around the house is good too. And with you here, I think I'm pretty well protected, don't you?"

"I sure hope so, but I won't rest until we find Mama, and you shouldn't either. Just thinking you're safe can be trouble. Be extra careful and even more aware of your surroundings every minute, hear?"

I could tell he was upset but chose not to extend our conversation. "Is Brian coming over? I want to tell you both about my interview with Mrs. Wellborn."

At mention of the name, Mike looked at me blankly. "Sally's neighbor," I added for clarification.

Mike said, "I just spoke with Brian before you came through the door. He said he was headed our way."

"Good," I responded as I picked up Sweet Pea and held her close. "I want to make sure that nothing happens to her either, understood?"

"Of course. The queen and her princess. And don't you dare ask me which one *you* are." he laughed. "I'll never confess."

I laughed with him. There was no doubt in my mind that he thought Sweet Pea was the queen, but maybe not. "When Brian gets here, let's just order takeout pizza for supper. Sound good? I'll make a salad to go with that too."

As the three of us sat munching our meal, I filled them in on what I had learned from Mrs. Wellborn.

"So Mama's the killer, then?" asked Mike.

"I don't think so. I had a vision of Mama in Sally's apartment, but they weren't alone—I saw a figure standing over Sally. Although I couldn't make him out, I know there's definitely a man involved in that murder. We just have to figure out who it was."

Both men sat with their own thoughts, and then I remembered I hadn't told them about the guard—the very man who had followed me along the path at Lake Las Vegas and into the mall—Tony had in place to "protect" me. After I relayed what had happened, Brian asked, "What did he look like again, Rosie?"

The description I gave them seemed to hit a nerve with Brian. "You've got to be kidding. I saw him at the lounge just the other night talking to Johnny. I had no idea he was the man you meant, Rosie." exclaimed Brian. "And he's working for Tony now, right under my nose?"

"Listen, I didn't actually know he worked for Tony until he said so today," I comforted him.

"I've got to do something about this reporter gig, because I'm not on top of my game at all to have missed this. And Mike, now that you can't help me out as much because you have to protect Rosie even more, I'm going to ask for the vacation time I've got coming from the news station so I can see what we can do to wrap this whole thing up."

"Don't be so hard on yourself, Brian. These guys have everything in place to stall us time after time again," Mike consoled.

"Thanks but no thanks for standing up for me. The truth is this has gone on for far too long. It's only by digging further that we're going to break this case, and you know it, my friend."

Mike just nodded his head reluctantly. "I suppose."

"What about Cindy?" I asked. "Is she in danger too?"

"I don't think so," answered Brian. "She's pretty much considered a part of the group there, and they seem to trust her. At least, Johnny does, which is saying something. It's you they're not sure of, and for good reason. After all, it was you who foiled their schemes."

"That's why it's so interesting to me that I'm still working at the lounge. And for that matter, it's interesting that Romano remains there too. But it makes sense just to keep things as they were before so it appears Mama is the only bad apple in the bunch. But I'm telling you, that's going to backfire for sure."

"What do you mean?" asked Mike.

"Because we all know now there are other people involved, it's not just Mama. And the truth always comes out sooner or later, right?"

"Pretty much," Mike responded.

We all sat there glumly, and then Brian asked Mike, "Did you meet with Melissa's roommate?"

"I could only get a few minutes alone with her. She said she had nothing to add to what she'd told Rosie, but then she said something interesting—'I'm curious, though. Did you ever find out more about who gave Melissa the diamond ring?' I didn't know what she was talking about, so I simply answered no. So tell me, what's this diamond ring she was talking about?"

I spoke up. "When I met with Mary and we went through Melissa's things, there was a jewelry box with a beautiful diamond ring. It looked like an engagement ring, to be exact. There was a note with it that read 'You are the one. Love, B.B.' We didn't know who could've given it to her. I thought it was David Masterly."

"Any reason?" asked Mike.

"Apparently, Melissa's nickname for him was Big Boy."

"You've got to be kidding!" exclaimed Mike with a chuckle, eying Brian, who blushed.

"Rosie, you still have the ring, don't you?" asked Brian.

"I do. Want me to get it?"

Both men nodded, and I rose to go upstairs. "There's more coffee there, so just help yourself. I'll be back in a minute."

As I reached into my hiding spot for the jewelry box, I thought of Melissa, who'd had high hopes of starting a new life—one filled with love. All that was left of her dream was now sitting in a box in my hand. That thought was depressing, and I was even more inspired to find her killer.

As I stepped back into the kitchen, I handed the box to Mike. "Here it is. Really beautiful, isn't it?" I asked as I took the ring out of the box and put it onto my own finger. I waved it around at the guys, who watched me in amusement.

"What are you going to do with it?" asked Mike.

"I'm hoping that we never have to report this, and I can sell it so I can send the money to Melissa's mother. It's got to be worth about $30,000, don't you think?" I asked as I flashed it in front of them.

Brian was watching me carefully, lost in thought. "I think that's a great idea, Rosie girl. Why didn't I think of that?"

"Selling it?" I asked.

"No, taking it into jewelry stores around town to find out where it was purchased and who bought it for Melissa. That's how we can prove who the real B.B. is."

Mike and I looked at each other in surprise. It was a great idea. Why hadn't we thought of it? Mike sat silently, never questioning why I hadn't turned it into the police. I guessed we all were in agreement that it would do us no good. After a few moments, Mike changed the subject. "Was Isabella okay with going back to Maria's?"

"Yes, and I was very proud of the way she handled it at the end in spite of my not giving her a choice. She looked so pretty with her new haircut, and she was so excited about her new things. I think she knew better than to push it with me."

Brian looked up and smiled. "By the way, your hair looks very nice. Not so … wild."

I returned his smile. For him to have even noticed was something, for he had been thoroughly engrossed in his dark thoughts. "Thanks, Cowboy."

I began to tell them about my fabulous hairdresser, Richard, but I noticed that both were tuning me out, so I said, "Well, guys, I'm going to clean up these dishes and head to bed. Will one of you please put Sweet Pea out and stay with her?"

They looked at each other, and it was Mike who rose from the table to take Sweet Pea outside. Then Brian stepped behind and leaned into me as I worked at the sink. "Just be careful, Rosie, and watch every step you take. You have a way of attracting dead bodies and all sorts of crazy stuff."

Instead of being pleased by his concern for me, I was somewhat frustrated, because I knew what he was saying was true—I did seem to attract trouble. I felt self-conscious about his attention to me and pushed him away. Teasingly, I said, "I think it's you who needs to be careful. Johnny doesn't like you *at all*, you know."

Just then Mike entered with Sweet Pea, who danced around Brian's feet. He was forced to tend to her, and Mike winked at me as he watched Brian bend down to play with the dog. He certainly knew who the queen was all right.

I left the guys strategizing and went upstairs to get ready for bed. When I stepped into the bathroom for my nightly chores, I was pleased to see my new haircut in the mirror. I'd definitely have to call Louie tomorrow and thank him for encouraging me to see Richard. As I looked more closely in the mirror, I could see my face change into one of horror, and I immediately jumped back, afraid. When I looked again, my face was normal. Another premonition. Oh no.

As I closed my eyes ready to drift off, I remembered I hadn't checked in with my girlfriends. I'd have to be sure to call Susannah tomorrow morning and tell her all about Isabella. I knew she'd get a kick out of Isabella's calling me Mama. It felt good to think of that, and I fell asleep with a smile on my face and Sweet Pea snuggled against to me.

CHAPTER 26

When I came downstairs in the morning, I could see Mike standing outside, guarding Sweet Pea while she did her morning chores. He looked relaxed, but he didn't fool me. No one else might notice how surreptitiously and alertly he looked around, but I did. It brought a smile to my face, and I thought how lucky I was to have him as my protector.

I grabbed a cup of coffee and headed into my office to call Susannah. When she answered, she responded with relief. "Girl, I'm glad you called. We all were wondering what's going on there."

I told her nothing much had changed at work. I wasn't about to tell her about the man Tony had "guarding" me, which I didn't for a moment think was just that. Instead, I diverted her with all that'd happened with Isabella.

"She sounds adorable," Susannah exclaimed. After a pause, she asked, "If it ever comes down to it, would you ever consider adopting her?"

I was taken somewhat off guard by her question, since I hadn't really considered it. "I don't know. Honestly, I don't even think it's a possibility, since they're trying to locate more of her relatives. The agency thinks it's always best for a child to remain within the family—even the extended family."

"Ohh, that's too bad," Susannah said.

I ignored the implications of her words and asked, "Speaking of family, how are your furry little ones? Do you have them yet?"

"No, not yet. We'll pick them up in a couple of days— they'll be ready sooner than we expected," she laughed. "We have new pictures of them I'll send you. Gosh, are they ever cute. Even Henry has pictures of them on his phone and is showing them off to people at work. Who would've thought he'd be so excited about them?"

I laughed at the image of that somewhat uptight, proper guy all excited about having puppies. We talked some more, and then it was time to say goodbye. "Don't be upset if I don't call every day. We agreed a call once a week would be enough unless something unexpected happens and I need your help. I'm in good hands, just not always available to talk."

"I know. It's important for you to remain in touch with us, though, so we don't go crazy with worry. I realize you can't be on such a tight schedule for a daily call—that would make things even more stressful for you."

"Thanks for understanding. Let the girls know all is well, please." And we hung up.

Mike peeked into the office and asked, "Do you want me to cook you breakfast, or are you going to have your special granola?"

"Thanks anyhow, Mike. I'll stick with my granola today."

I fixed my cereal and joined Mike at the table, where he was sipping his coffee and reading the local newspaper. "I guess I'm going to have to meet with Tony today and see what's up with this 'guard' he has protecting me. What do you think my approach should be?" I asked.

He lowered the paper and looked over it at me, concerned. "Why do *you* think he has that man following you? Any ideas?"

"Not really. I can't believe he's concerned about my safety per se. Maybe he thinks I know more than I do about what he's been involved in or thinks I have those papers Melissa took."

"Have you thought that maybe he's having you guarded for someone else, perhaps B.B.?"

"Oh my, that makes more sense, doesn't it?"

Mike just stared at me, deep in thought. "Rosie, it looks like we never gave much thought to your involvement beyond your simply using your psychic abilities to help us. Brian and I are amazed that you are so deep into our investigation because you're legally not part of it. But there you are—right smack-dab in the middle of things, and you seem to attract all of it to you."

"You all keep saying that, yet, isn't it possible I'm meant to be involved, that it's because of me that we've been able to move this case further than ever before?" I sputtered, defensively. I continued, "That should be good enough. And you know darned well I'm going to do what I can to bring whoever murdered Melissa and Sally to justice. I feel somewhat responsible for their deaths, and I'm not going to rest until all this comes to the proper end. So with you or without you, I'm moving forward with this," I proclaimed.

"Now, Rosie, calm down ..."

"And if I'm not legally a part of this investigation, maybe you should make me a legal part of it."

"I'm not sure that's possible, but ..."

"Until then, *Mister* Mike, I'd advise you not to look a gift horse in the mouth," I snapped at him as I rose from the table, leaving him looking stunned. He'd never been on the receiving end of my temper before.

I stood over the table glowering at him, and the tension between us rose to new heights. As I scurried from the room, he called, "But ...?"

I knew I could be impossible to deal with at times, but c'mon, it didn't take a rocket scientist for either of them to realize that once you asked someone for help, you never knew how that was going to play out. I was on edge, for something was going to pop soon, and I didn't have a clue what it was. But I could feel it in my bones.

Upstairs, I glanced down at my bare feet and decided to see whether I could get an early pedicure by Elanya. I smiled thinking of her, for she is one smart woman. She'd set herself apart from the other spas in town and became an instant success by offering early-morning pedicures so women and men could have them done before they went off to work. Then, as her business grew, she took over the space next door and added a section where clients could sit in lounge chairs or at a café table and enjoy a variety of imported coffees and teas.

As if that weren't enough, she knew that everyone who came into her spa needed to avoid stress in order to begin the day in the right frame of mind. She charged $2 for inexpensive, disposable earphones (or clients could bring their own) and the use of one of her many CD players, where you could listen to soothing music while sipping your drink of choice. You could even take a short nap in one of her lounge chairs. She donated the money she collected to her favorite charity. Her business had grown to the point she'd now taken over another space so she could accommodate more clients.

Elanya was an inspiration to anyone going into business. I was one of her first customers and one of the first speakers in her scheduled monthly "reset" talks. I spoke about the importance of meditation, which, she told me later, had given her the idea of selling CD time. She'd never forgotten that I was instrumental in helping her create that aspect of her business, and she allowed me to be squeezed into her busy schedule when necessary.

After I telephoned her, I went down to the kitchen to tell Mike I was going to take a quick shower and then have a pedicure. "You don't have to come with me, you know. This is something I can do by myself."

"Or NOT," he responded with some irritation. "No, I'll come with you."

"Have you ever had a pedicure?" I asked.

"No, why?"

"I'll treat you to one today. We'll have them together."

He looked at me in surprise, but seemed to think better of questioning me. "I guess so, if that means that I can keep you in sight, which *is* my priority, after all."

I knew Mike was a bit annoyed, but I wasn't going to let it bother me. I turned away and hid a smile at the thought of him in a spa chair having a pedicure. This should be fun, I thought, and it certainly would be different.

When we got there, Elanya was finishing up with a customer. She greeted us with a cheery hello and nodded her head toward the bottles of nail polish lined up in a container hanging on the wall. "Hey, beautiful, pick your color, please. Your chairs are waiting," she said, nodding toward two chairs with water running into their basins. She'd be doing my pedicure; one of her helpers would be doing Mike's.

As I climbed into my seat, I smiled and nodded hello to the woman next to me, whose pedicure was just beginning too. She smiled back, then shyly leaned toward me. "Are you the woman who helped those little girls escape? You were so brave," she said in a soft, conspiratorial voice.

I felt my face grow hot. I turned away and simply gave her a tight smile and three quick nods. She continued, "I swear my neighbor is into all that stuff. He says it's his niece who's staying with him, but I don't believe that for a minute. Now another niece has come to stay."

She had my full attention now, and I turned to her. "Is he married?" I asked, curious.

"He was, but his wife left him. They were continually having rows, with lots of screaming and arguing."

"Who's your neighbor?" I asked, fully alert now to what she was saying.

"He's with Channel 5 news, but I can't remember his name." She paused. "A senior moment, I guess, but you'd know him if you heard his name."

My heart pounded. Surely she didn't mean Brian, did she? How ridiculous, I scolded myself. "Is he on the air?" I asked, my interest mounting

"Oh, no, he's in charge there." Leaning still closer, she whispered, "And he has parties quite often with other bigwigs in town."

"Like who?" I asked, now completely captivated by what she was telling me.

She began to name some of them, and I recognized a few. Then she said, "Even when the police show up there, nothing happens."

My heart began to pound as I asked, "Have you ever seen the chief of police there?"

"Oh, yes indeed."

Mike called my name, but I turned toward him and held a finger in the air to signal a pause. "What did you say your name was? Maybe we could have coffee together some time. Please give me your telephone number, and I'll put it into my cell phone so I won't forget it," I said as I reached for my bag.

She obliged, and after I had added her number, I turned back to Mike with a smile. "I just love going to the spa, you meet the nicest people."

He looked at me and smiled, despite looking ill at ease sitting there while someone fussed with his feet. He leaned closer to me and whispered with concern, "I don't have to wear nail polish, do I?" and then stated in a firm voice, "I'm not willing to do that."

I laughed and patted his hand. "Nooo. Men usually leave their toenails free of polish so they don't turn yellow, so you're all set, Mike. My polish will take just a few more minutes to dry, then we can leave."

He looked relieved. I wondered whether he'd tell Brian about his salon experience or try to keep it to himself. It was too bad he might not have a choice, because I'd have to explain to Brian how I'd obtained this new information—and when I did, it sure would be interesting to watch Brian's face. I sighed and sat back in my chair, closed my eyes, and tried to push aside everything spinning around in my head.

As we were leaving, I had to chuckle, for there's something about going into a spa or beauty parlor, because, thanks to the clients and staff, it's hard to leave without having learned something you didn't know before entering—some things good; others, not so much.

CHAPTER 27

I arrived at work early, and as I passed Tony's office, the man who was supposedly guarding me was talking to Tony, who was seated behind his desk. Without warning, I felt something snap inside me and fury build. I immediately turned back and marched into Tony's office, right up to the man who'd been following me. I poked his chest with my finger and turned to Tony. "What the heck is this man doing following me? What are you up to, Tony?"

Both men were startled and silent for a few seconds, until Tony reacted. "How dare you come into my office and speak to me that way," he bellowed.

Unfazed, I continued, "I want to know why you have this man following *me*."

When Tony saw I had no fear of him, he paused and backtracked a bit. "Now Rosalie, you need to calm down.

I'm doing you a favor, that's all. You know Mama's missing, don't you? I'm sure you're aware that she was pretty upset with you and even threatened to harm you, right? Now, we don't want that to happen …"

At that very moment, it all became clear. That's exactly why Tony had me followed—not to protect me but in the hopes that Mama will come after me and they'd be able to capture *her*. They were afraid she'd spill the beans if she got into the wrong hands before they found her, and they'd all go down. Maybe in the beginning it was about the missing pages, but right now, I knew without a doubt they were using me to trap Mama.

As I was coming out of my trance, Tony asked, "What's the matter with you? Didn't you hear what I said?"

I hesitated before answering him because I needed to decide how to respond. I wasn't sure whether I should back down and apologize or continue to confront him. It would serve no purpose for me to remain angry, so I played contrite and dumb. "Oh, gosh, I didn't think of it that way."

"Remember, you're family now, Rosalie," he added in a tone full of innuendo.

I felt a chill wash over me with the thought of what he'd meant, which only made me angry again. "I know you think you're doing me a favor, Tony, but don't worry about me—my boyfriend can protect me. Just tell your man to stay away from me. I told him before that if he didn't, I'd call the cops on him, and I mean it."

Tony was silent long enough for me to make my escape. Two could play at this game, I thought. Maybe I'd make myself accessible to Mama to make sure she'd be in our hands, not Tony's, as lord knew what they'd do to her, I thought.

I hurried to the employee's lounge to place my bag in my locker, and there at the table was Shirley, with tears in her eyes. I gave her a questioning look, and she smiled weakly and said, "The same old thing. My boyfriend wants me to quit." She pushed her cell phone away from her with disgust and folded her arms in front of her. "I'm not going to do it. I want a beautiful wedding, and this is the only way I'm going to get enough money to have it. I don't know why he doesn't get this—I'm doing it for *us*."

The vision I had received on her first day of work at the lounge came flooding back to me, leaving me chilled. I'd seen her lying on the floor with blood pooling all around her and someone standing over her with a gun. "How much longer do you need to work to raise the money you need?" I asked, hoping it would be just a few weeks.

"Another couple of months, at least."

"You know, Shirley, you can have a beautiful wedding without spending a lot of money. One of my dearest friends had just a few people at hers, which was in a glorious setting ..."

"You're just like all the people who think I don't deserve to have a big, beautiful wedding, isn't that right?"

"Oh, no, Shirley, that's not it at all. All I'm saying is that you don't need to spend a lot of money for a wedding, because it's really all about you and your man, not those who attend the wedding."

"Listen, I know you're trying to help, but I'm not going to quit here yet," she declared with determination.

"Just be careful not to get your man too angry," I warned. "You can push them just so far, you know."

"I know—he's already warned me."

"I don't like the sound of that. Please just promise me you'll think about what I said, okay?"

"Okay, I will," she responded without enthusiasm. It was obvious she'd heard it all before.

Sometimes there's just so much one can do to change someone else's mind. We all have to do things our own way, for isn't that how we learn? I arrived at the front desk eager to get back to some sense of routine. So far, this day was not even close to that, and it was beginning to wear on me.

I was fortunate because it turned out to be a fairly slow evening. Mimi came out to check on me just before my break. "How are you, Rosie? Things okay here?"

"So far, so good," I answered with a smile.

"I heard you had words with Tony. Anything I should know about?"

I wasn't sure how to answer Mimi but decided honesty was the best policy. "Are you aware that Tony is having me followed?"

"What do you mean, followed?" she asked, furrowing her brow.

I could tell she wasn't aware of it, which pleased me. "Tony said that since Mama is missing, he was having me 'guarded' so she can't hurt me."

Seeing her puzzled expression, I continued, "You may not know that Mama threatened to get even with me at the time I exposed the plot with the little girls. She was absolutely furious with me and tried to put the blame on me."

"Do you believe she'd actually harm you?" asked Mimi with concern.

"Yes, I do," I stated flatly before asking, "Don't you?"

Mimi slowly nodded her head, deep in thought. "Yes. As long as I've known her, she's always been angry about something. She's one of those glass-half-empty people."

I decided not to say anything about my theory of why Tony was having me followed, yet, I wanted to make my feelings clear. "I don't like the feeling of being followed, and I don't want him to guard me. Isn't there anything you can do about that?"

"Actually, I feel comfortable knowing you are being guarded, since things are so much up in the air. Sorry, but I think it's a good idea. I'll have a talk with Tony, though."

I continued, "Besides, my boyfriend is always there protecting me. I don't need anyone else to do that."

Mimi didn't respond, although I believe she thought it a bit odd Tony had me under guard. Tony certainly was an odd one. Curiosity overcame me, and I asked, "What was your Tony like as a kid?"

Although Mimi seemed surprised by my question, she gamely answered, "He's quite a bit older than I am, so all I remember about him is that he was a bully—but he wasn't actually the bully himself—he had someone else do his dirty work. He used to amaze me, for he's always had the ability to find someone to be at his beck and call."

We stood together for several more moments, and I felt the urge to ask, "Have you decided whether to close this place or keep it open?"

Mimi eyed me thoughtfully and asked, "Would it matter to you?"

"Not really," I responded, honestly.

"Well, I don't have an answer for you at this time. I'm still trying to clean up everything that's happened these last few weeks."

When Bambi came to relieve me for my break, I watched Mimi's expression change for she obviously wasn't a fan of hers. In turn, Bambi stiffened in Mimi's presence.

I watched them glaring at each other and decided to break the mood by saying, "I'm off; I'll be back soon. Are you hungry?" I asked Mimi. "Want to join me for a break? I don't think Romano would mind."

"No, thank you. That's okay, you go ahead, though."

We ended up walking together until we reached Romano's kitchen, where we parted. Mimi headed down the hallway, and out of the corner of my eye, I thought I saw her enter Tony's office.

CHAPTER 28

❦ Hey there, Romano," I called out with enthusiasm. "How are you doing tonight, my dear friend?" I was always happy to be there where I found release from the stress of working at the lounge.

He smiled at me. "And you, my dear Rosebud, how are you?" he asked as he gave me full kisses on both cheeks.

"Glad to me here," I happily responded.

As he eyed me, he asked, worry flitting across his features, "What's going on?"

"Basically, the same old thing. I guess I'm just getting tired of it all."

"Come sit. I've made you a cold salad of shrimp, avocado, mango, fresh greens, and a new fruit dressing. Tell me what you think."

I swooned with the first bite. "How do you do it, Romano? Each new thing you feed me is better than the

last, but don't take me wrong, I love *everything* you create."
I patted my belly, which was beginning to round a bit.
Outside his kitchen, I'd have to be careful about what I put
into my mouth so I wouldn't put on excess weight.

Romano looked pleased as he watched me thoroughly
enjoy what he'd placed in front of me. Between mouthfuls,
I said, "By the way, I asked Mimi if she is going to close
down the lounge, and she said she'd didn't know yet. If she
does, what will you do?"

"I've had plenty of time to think about it, actually. My
being here was always meant to be an opportunity to
try out and test some of my recipes. I've always wanted
to have my own place, and I've got enough money saved
that I think I can. I've also collected a number of customers
whom I think would support it," he added, pleased with
himself.

"Wow, that's great. Have you got a name for your
restaurant yet?"

"Not yet. Any ideas?"

"No, but I'll think about it."

"What about you, Rosebud? What'll you do? Back to
writing?"

I nodded my head slowly. Although I've always enjoyed
writing, I knew deep inside that since I'd been involved
with these murders and child trafficking, writing wouldn't
be enough; I would always want to do more. Being so
involved with everything that had happened and was still
going on wasn't anything I'd anticipated, but it felt good to
be climbing out of my self-made shell and spreading my
wings more than I ever had.

Romano rose to stir something on the stove, while I
sat with my thoughts. Unexpectedly, Mimi appeared in
the doorway. She said a cheery hello to Romano and then

asked, "Rosie, will you please come into my office for a minute before you go back out front?"

"Sure, I'm just about finished here. I'll be right there."

Mimi simply waved to Romano before leaving. He asked, "Is everything okay?"

After I told him about my earlier conversation with her about my 'guard,' he brought forth some cookies he'd made and asked, "Would you mind delivering these to her when you go? Of course, this one on top is for you right now," he added as he saw me salivating over them.

When I entered Mimi's office with the plate of cookies, she smiled and said, "Romano's cookies are the best, aren't they? Every now and then, I find a plate of them on my desk. I love them too much to ask him to stop doing that," she laughed as she lightly patted her stomach.

I laughed with her, knowing I wouldn't be able to say no to them either. "You wanted to see me?" I asked.

"Yes. Please sit down. This will only take a minute. I went to see Tony after our conversation to see where he was in all this, because something wasn't adding up. We don't usually place a guard on anyone if there's a problem, and I began to wonder, why you? Yes, I know Mama threatened you and all, but it still didn't make sense. Tony flatly refused to talk to me about it other than to say he felt under obligation to make sure that Mama doesn't hurt you. He said it would be bad for business if that happened, and I had to agree with him on that aspect. Don't you?"

"Yes, I guess so. It wouldn't really benefit anyone if I were hurt, much less have the lounge make the papers again with another incident. But I'm unhappy with that man following me around. Who is he, anyway?"

"He's one of Tony's old-time bullies, although I think he's fairly harmless. He's not the sharpest knife in the drawer, if you catch my drift. His name is Lorenzo Mastrionni." She looked steadily at me, "I think there's more to this whole thing than meets the eye. Anything you want to share?"

I remained silent, for what could I say? I returned to the front desk, where Bambi was deep in conversation with Johnny. I could tell by the way she was leaning into him that she cared about him. In turn, he pulled her into his arms and whispered something in her ear, which made her laugh. When I stepped forward, I startled both of them, and they hurriedly pulled apart. Johnny immediately turned away and headed to the front door. Bambi faced me with flushed cheeks and asked, "Isn't he darling?"

"He's one of a kind, all right," I answered since "darling" wouldn't be a word I'd use to describe him.

Bambi gave me a big hug. "See you tomorrow, Rosie. Have a good night."

As I hugged her back, a strange feeling overcame me. I wanted to protect her, but from what?

The rest of my shift was a drag, and I was grateful when Cindy showed up. She looked refreshed after her night off. Her cheeks were pink, and her eyes sparkled. "Hey, girlfriend, what have you been up to? You look dazzling."

"You're not going to believe this, but I got a call from an old boyfriend who's in town for business, and we had such a good time yesterday. It was amazing how easy it was for us to reconnect, almost as if no time had passed." She smiled, "It was really nice."

I hugged her. "I'm so glad for you. Is he still here?"

"Yes. We're going to get together again later. He wants to dine at Mon Ami Gabi and watch Bellagio's water show from the balcony."

"May I ask whether he's married?"

"No, thank God," she laughed.

"Better not let Johnny see you with another man—although as much as he doesn't like Brian, he'd probably be glad you have someone new." We chuckled, and as if by magic, Brian walked through the door, which made us laugh even harder.

Behind him came Mike, and Cindy and I reacted in different ways at seeing him—yet for the same reason. He was a very attractive man. In fact, both he and Brian were. How had this become so complicated? We stood and talked for a few minutes. Both guys were in a good mood, and Brian asked me, "Do you want to join us for a drink in the bar?"

At my surprise, Mike reassured me, "If you don't want to, you don't have to. It's entirely up to you," he added expansively.

I had a nagging sense I should leave, but I could see how much they wanted me to join them, so I relented. "Why not?"

It was no joy for me to be there as a customer, even if only for a cocktail, but it was important to keep up the appearance Mike and I had a relationship. Once inside, I ignored the girls who were dancing and headed to the corner table farthest away from it all. It was good to be sitting here with Brian, because I spent most of my time with Mike. Brian seemed to feel the same way, for he leaned forward and said, "Hey, Rosie girl, everything okay?"

I smiled. "It will be when all of this mess is cleared up. Anything new from your end?"

"Not really, all is quiet. Can't seem to get a location for Mama. Wherever she's hiding, she's doing a good job of it."

"That's too bad."

Mike came to the table with a tray of our drinks. I took one sip from mine and decided I'd better get my purse now, before I forgot about it. Besides, I wanted to freshen my lipstick and pull my hair back into a ponytail instead of having it sticking out all over the place. "Excuse me, guys. I'll be right back. I'm just going to get my purse."

They looked up as I rose, and Brian said, "Hurry back; we don't want to lose sight of you for too long."

It felt good to know both would be waiting for me when I returned. I took my time walking to the employee lounge and let myself relax a bit. When I tried to open the door, I had to push hard because something was blocking it. As I finally made my way in, I was grabbed and shoved forward. I nearly lost my balance but regained it before bumping into the table—where I was stunned to see Bambi sitting there. She was tied to one of the chairs, her arms behind her. Thick tape was across her mouth, and she wore a terrified expression.

Shirley was in the other chair, in the same condition but with tears rolling down her face. She kept trying to talk through the tape, but everything she said was muffled, though we could make out some of what she was saying.

"No, no, Kevin, don't. I'll quit ..." she pleaded as she nodded her head up and down.

He poked me with his shotgun and ordered me to sit down. "You all are nothing but sluts. Do you think I want you now, Shirley, after you've been selling your body here?" he shouted, spraying spittle.

Shirley nodded her head. "Please ..." she begged. She began to rock her chair back and forth, and her face became mottled with sweat and tears as fury built.

"Hey, cut that out." Kevin shouted. He turned and stepped toward her, aiming the gun at her head. Then, surprisingly, he began to cry big gulping sobs as he yelled at Shirley, "You deserve to die, you bitch."

Shirley became hysterical and rocked her chair back and forward to get farther and farther away from him. He moaned, "We could have had a wonderful life together, you know."

He had forgotten all about Bambi and me for the moment, but suddenly he swung the shotgun around and aimed it at me. "Don't do anything foolish, Kevin." I pleaded, this can all be worked out." I got up from my chair and stepped toward him. "Give me the gun, Kevin, now," I ordered. "Hand it over, now," I shouted again, with as much authority as I could muster.

This caused him to hesitate for a second to weigh his decision. "No way, bitch. No one is going to take me down. The world would be better off without the three of you sluts anyway. You all deserve to die. You take in kids— kids like Shirley—and change them into whores. Who does that? What kind of people are you, anyway?" he asked as he looked back and forth between Bambi and me.

Kevin pointed the gun at each one of us and pretended to shoot us, yelling "Pow!" each time. It was one of the most terrifying experiences I'd ever had, and we all became rattled as we watched Kevin get more and more out of control.

I had to do something quickly before it became impossible to stop him. All of a sudden I yelled, "Who's there? Don't come in right now," pretending someone was at the door.

Kevin jerked around, confused about what was going on, and hollered, "Who's there?" and stepped closer to the door—where I was now standing.

That is when I made my move. Thank God for my karate lessons, because with a right arm swing and a kick up, I caught him off guard. He had just swung around to

213

face me again and didn't expect me to knock the gun from his hand. As I did, there was an earsplitting noise and then a crash as the chair Shirley was sitting on spun backward and fell onto the floor with her still tied to it.

When Kevin saw this, he raced to Shirley's side. "Oh, my god. No. No."

Shirley was lying in a pool of blood just as I'd seen in my vision—but this time, the blood was coming from a superficial head injury, the type that always created a bloody scene. Shirley was alive but completely hysterical.

Just then the door was thrown open by Brian and Mike, who had come to check on me because I'd taken way too long to return to the table. When they saw me and grasped some of what had taken place, both of them looked at me and rolled their eyes. "Take Kevin into custody," I ordered. "I'll explain in a minute. I've got to make sure Bambi and Shirley are all right."

When I saw Brian head to Shirley to offer first aid until help could arrive, I went to Bambi to untie her. Mike was calling both an ambulance and the police.

As I undid the tape around Bambi's mouth, she let out an anguished sound and began to cry even harder. I untied her hands from behind the chair, and she clung to me and wouldn't let go as we clutched one another. I held her tight and told her I loved her, and she looked at me, unable to speak, and just nodded in agreement.

Just then, Johnny pushed into the room and rushed to where Bambi and I were standing. As soon as Bambi saw him, she pulled away from me and ran into his arms. "Rosie saved my life, Johnny, she saved my life ..."

Johnny looked at me with such love and gratitude that I knew he'd never forget what I'd done, which sometimes changed lives forever.

Death at the Lake

As soon as Mike got off the phone, he came to me and held me tight. He leaned down and wiped several tears from my face. Brian saw this and hurriedly turned Shirley over to the medics, who had just arrived, and came to us. Then Mike stepped away, and it was Brian who held me close to him now, murmuring, "You all right, babe?" I nodded yes and stood back after a minute or so.

I looked at both of them with some annoyance, as they were looking at each other with the same expression each had worn when they had first walked through the door and saw what was happening. I could see it in their eyes— how does she do it? Always getting herself involved like this? I simply warned them, "Don't say a word, either one of you. I don't want to hear it."

The night was long. Apparently, Shirley, not realizing what Kevin was up to, had let him in through the back entrance. Bambi had startled them in the employee lounge and became trapped there. It was the old game that we humans unwittingly play sometimes when we are in a power struggle and let it go too far. This, of course, was an extreme case.

Kevin was handcuffed and led away; he'd be taken to the state hospital and tested for mental stability. He left sobbing, repeating over and over again, "I didn't mean to hurt anyone. I just wanted Shirley back ..."

Shirley was taken to the hospital to be treated and spend the night; her parents had been contacted and were supposedly on their way there. Most likely, her days at the lounge were over, and there would be no wedding.

Johnny sat with Bambi and glowered at anyone who upset her in any way, especially the police who questioned her. Then he took her away while whispering sweet nothings to calm her down.

215

Cindy sat with me and held my hand as I told the police my version of what had happened. She knew how much I hated dealing with the police, and she made them keep my questioning brief.

Brian and Mike were doing their own investigation, which irritated the police, who tried in vain to order them to leave, but because they had come upon the scene shortly after the shooting, they were an integral part of the investigation. Neither could the police do much about Brian's gathering information for a firsthand report for the news station.

Mimi was supportive in all ways and demanded I take the next day off, which I was not about to do. It wouldn't be fair to Cindy, and it would be better for me to keep busy. Once I retrieved my purse, Mike and I drove home in silence. I felt drained, and there really was nothing left to say.

When we got home, Mike took care of Sweet Pea, while I raced upstairs and threw myself across my bed. I cried gulping sobs, releasing all my resentment of all the turmoil in my life. *"Oh, Gram, I just hate what's happening around me,"* I wailed. *"I just hate it."*

I smelled her first, then I heard her voice. *"It's okay to cry, darling Rosie. It's good to connect to your feelings and cry about all the ways humans continually hurt each other. If only we were able to weep enough tears of remorse to drown all the ugly hate in this world, wouldn't that be wonderful? For now, Rosie, know that the love within you is stronger than any negative feelings, so never hold back your love for all you are and have in this lifetime, understand?"*

I felt like the little girl I used to be, with my head in her lap all the times I cried and needed her support. Just like she had back then, I swore I could feel her stroke my hair. I sighed with pleasure and fell into a deep sleep.

CHAPTER 29

When I awoke the next morning, I found myself still in my clothes with covers thrown over me. Mike must have placed them there and put Sweet Pea in bed with me. She now stood over me and watched my every move with worried eyes, and I rolled onto my back and let the memories of yesterday flow through me. I held up my hands to look at my nails to check my new polish, though it seemed ages ago, not just yesterday, that Mike and I had been at the spa. I recalled the conversation with the woman sitting next to me and realized I hadn't even told the others about it yet.

I stretched, then tossed the covers over my head to make Sweet Pea think this was playtime, so she nosed under them and began to lick my face and toss the covers aside. I had to smile, for she was determined to make a tunnel out of them, and she kept flopping them up and over her tiny body.

I didn't feel like getting up and facing the day, but I knew I couldn't put it off much longer. Just then, Brian telephoned to make sure I was okay. I was determined to get back to business, and so I asked, "Cowboy, what do you know about your boss, the manager of the station?"

"Funny you should ask, because I just received an anonymous tip about him this morning. It was something else—it accused him of being in the human trafficking business and more, bad business for sure."

Brian hesitated before asking, "I'm wondering if it could be from Mama. Maybe she's trying to tighten up the case against the others who were involved with her. What do you think, Rosie? Anything come to you?"

I closed my eyes and let my thoughts drift. I saw Mama sitting at a desk typing away on a computer, but I couldn't be sure what she was doing. "It's possible, but it just doesn't feel right."

I told Brian what the woman who sat next to me at the spa had said. There was a pause afterward, and out of the blue, he asked, "Was Mike with you at the spa?"

"Yes, of course."

"Ah," he responded, "Tell Mike to give me a call when we're through, please."

I wondered what that was all about. It was only later when I heard Mike laughing and telling Brian to buzz off that I knew Brian was teasing him for being at the spa with me. It guess it was a 'guy thing' between the two of them.

Later, when it was time for me to go to work and we were on our way, Mike was acting more than professional; he was almost standoffish. Even when he opened the door for me at the lounge, he gave me just a perfunctory kiss on the cheek. It was almost as if he were going overboard to show me he didn't care. I looked at him and said, "You're going to have to do better than that, buddy, or anyone seeing us is going to think we've argued."

He bit back a smile and gave me a light kiss on the forehead, which was not quite what I'd expected but better than nothing. I was early, and just the thought of going into the employee lounge made me queasy, for I could still envision Bambi tied up at the table with terror on her face. In my mind, I could also picture Shirley lying on the floor with blood pooling all around her, so instead of heading down the hallway, I popped in to see dear Romano. As soon as he saw me, he came over and looked me up and down, almost as if to make sure I was all right. "Come, my darling, and see what I'm concocting. I think you're going to love it. It should be done in time for your break."

He grabbed my hand and led me to the stove. I could already smell the chicken cooking, and I began to salivate. "It's going to be old-fashioned chicken and biscuits, but with crispy pieces of chicken that have been separately floured and lightly fried in these wonderful spices." Romano kissed the tips of his fingers, flung his hand out and looked at me. We both laughed. I sure did love that man.

I sailed through my evening and break time with Romano, my thoughts on Mike. What was going on with him? When Cindy arrived so I could take a break, she seemed to be floating along. "Oh my, look at you—you look like the cat that swallowed the canary." I said.

"Oh, Rosebud, I think I'm in love. That man and I had one sweet time."

"It sure looks like it—you're grinning from ear to ear."

"He's even canceled his flight home, and he's going to stay for a few more days just to be with me. Where's Mimi? I've got to see if I can take the next two nights off. Do you think she'll let me?"

"I don't know, but you'll find out soon enough. Remind her of all the extra time you've put in, and I think you've got a chance."

As Cindy looked at me, she blurted out, "You okay? Glad to have your shift over?"

You bet," I answered.

Just then, Mike arrived, and it was interesting to see that Cindy didn't fuss over him in her usual way. She didn't even call out, "Hey, handsome." Instead, she hurried away in search of Mimi.

"Your chariot awaits," Mike teased, seeming to be in a better frame of mind. "Where is Cindy off to in such a hurry?"

"She's trying to get the next few nights off. She's in love."

Mike looked surprised but all he said was, "Good for her."

Mimi came out front, with Cindy behind her silently mouthing, "Please, please, please."

"Hi, Rosalie," Mimi greeted me. "Do you think you could stay one hour after your shift for the next several days? That'd give me time to do the accounting for your shift and have coverage here while I do that."

I looked at Cindy's happy face and said, "Sure."

Both Mimi and Cindy looked pleased. "Who's going to take over Cindy's shift?" I asked.

"I am," said Mimi. "It's about time I do a full night shift anyway to see what goes on here. That'll help me evaluate what I do with this place."

Once again, Mimi impressed me. She was certainly a smart businesswoman, and I had to admire her ability to allow someone some well-earned happy time off even at the expense of her own free time.

"Well, now that's settled, I guess it's time for me to get this night started," exclaimed Cindy as she hugged me and whispered, "I'm so happy. Thanks for helping out."

Cindy pulled away from me, and when she saw Mike, she said, "Hi there, handsome. How goes it?" with less than her normal enthusiasm.

"Not bad. How about you?" he asked.

"Things are great."

"Glad to hear it. Ready, Rosie?" he asked, stiffly.

I answered, "Sure, let's go home."

Cindy looked at us and seemed to sense things were off, but she never said a word. "Have a wonderful time off, Cindy," I hollered over my shoulder. "Have fun."

We rode home in an uncomfortable silence until I asked him, "Are you okay? You sure haven't been yourself lately."

"Yes, sorry. I've had a lot of my mind."

"Oh?"

"Yup." When he saw me frown, he added, "We're good though, right?"

I patted his arm. "For sure."

"Good." That's all he said before he began to whistle a somewhat somber tune. Yes, indeed, tomorrow was another day, and maybe then he'd tell me what was going on.

CHAPTER 30

E arly the next morning, Brian arrived in time for coffee. He was greeted by Sweet Pea, who was excited to see him, but was less enthusiastic than usual. She'd had a restless night, what with all my tossing and turning, and she was still tired. I hadn't showered yet and was looking more than a little scruffy, and Mike didn't look much better. Neither of us had rested well.

When Brian looked at us, he casually asked, "Late night?"

Mike answered, "Aren't they all?"

Brian said in a rush, "I just received another email this morning tipping me off that tonight is going to be a big night at my boss's house. The style of writing makes me believe the email is from the same person as before, so I'm thinking it's gonna be the real deal. Since I want you with me tonight, Mike, I'll call in someone else to watch over you, Rosie, okay?"

Mike hesitated for just a second before asking, "Who are you going to get?"

"I was thinking of asking Steve. Why?"

"I dunno if he's the best person. What do you think, Rosie?"

"I think you both are overacting and underestimating my ability to take care of myself. However, if it pleases you, have Steve pick me up at work and drop me off at home. Once we're here, we'll check all the locks, and if all is okay, I want him to leave. I don't want anyone else in my house tonight. I've been through enough trauma at work lately, and I want to come home and relax, which won't happen with anyone new here—and God knows I need my sleep. Deal?" I asked.

Both men wore expressions of doubt. I stood my ground saying, "That's the way it has to be. End of discussion."

Knowing how stubborn I can be, both seemed at a loss for how to best handle the situation. Finally, Mike said, "Agreed only if Steve remains outside doing his own surveillance. Okay with you, Brian?"

Brian nodded his head. "Not much else we can do, I guess."

I went to take my shower and dress for the day. As I walked into my bedroom, I smelled Gram and saw the red roses of love she always sends me, but that was it, nothing more. I guess she just wanted me to know she was here for me.

When I met Mike downstairs, he said, "Now, about tonight, you have to promise me you'll be careful. I don't like having to be away at this time, but there's really nothing I can do about it, so just promise me, all right?"

I nodded my head. "I promise," I said, wondering why he was fussing over me.

After I grabbed granola and fruit for breakfast, I went into my office to write my next spiritual column for *Women Living Well*. I tended to be paranoid about not having enough material for my articles, so I wrote down ideas and developed them enough to be able to get the flavor of what I wanted to say, and then I put them into a folder on my computer, where I had at least a dozen partially completed articles. This made it easy for me to pull one of them from the pile to flush it out and finish it. So far, this had worked out for me, yet, as I sat down to finish this article, it was hard not to let my mind wander. I was going to be the happiest girl alive when everything surrounding the Purple Passion Lounge, especially solving Melissa's and Sally's murders, was tied up. And maybe somehow all that would clear Jeff's name. We'd see.

Before long, it was early afternoon, and I heard Steve out front honking the horn for my ride to work. Mike's car was gone. I walked out and hopped into Steve's car. "Hi there, Steve, how goes it?"

"SOS. You know, same old stuff. It's nice to see you again, Rosie. I hear you've been through the ringer at work. Bet you'll be glad when this is all over, right?"

"You have no idea, Steve," I answered, smiling at the thought.

"Buckle up, and let's get you to work," he ordered.

Steve was a nice man, someone I liked, yet, I didn't feel as safe with him as I might. That probably came from the time my girlfriends and I had been out at Lake Las Vegas and we'd ended up on a crazy ride when the driver turned out not to be Steve as expected but someone who'd threatened us. Oh well, time to let bygones be bygones, I scolded myself.

When I arrived at work, Steve got out of the car and opened the door for me. It wasn't the same without Mike, and I missed him. Once again, I was a bit early and chose to see Romano before I clocked in. As I was headed his way, I heard a disturbance down the hallway. Curiosity got the better of me, and I headed toward the raised voices. I stood silent outside Tony's office door and listened to him and Johnny.

"Tony, I'm telling you, B.B. is saying that Mama is out of control and needs to be found ASAP. He thinks she's beginning to set a trap for all of us, and we both know she's smart enough to do that. Fuck. How are we going to find her?"

"Well, we have Rosalie being followed, right?"

"That's not enough, and you know it. We need to flush out Mama somehow," Johnny said.

"And how, I might ask, do you intend to do that?"

"How about we grab Rosalie's boyfriend? That might bring Mama out and offer a way for her to get back at Rosalie."

"That idea is pretty thin, but let's find out where he is today. Doesn't he usually drop Rosalie off for work? Call Lorenzo and see what he knows," ordered Tony.

"Will do. I'll be back after I get things ready for the girls to go on."

Since I didn't have time to hide, I pretended I was just coming in to work by hurriedly retreating a few steps and heading down the hallway again. Johnny seemed startled to see me but smiled and said, "Hi, Rosalie. You just getting in?"

"Yes, I like to get here a little early and say hi to Romano."

"Okay, then." Ever since Bambi had been tied up and in danger but I had saved her, Johnny had been treating me with kindness (for him). "You can clock in early if you'd like."

"Thanks, Johnny," I responded, grateful that he didn't ask me whether I'd heard anything he and Tony had said. I hurried down to the employee lounge and called Mike, who didn't answer his phone, which forced me to leave a voice mail message. What is it with these guys not answering their phones?

"Hi, Mike, just to let you know, Tony is up to no good. I'm warning you to be on the lookout. I overheard him and Johnny talking about finding out where *you* are so they can grab you and hold you for ransom because they hope that'll bring Mama to them. I'll try to get back to you if I hear anything more. Just *be careful*."

I had enough time left to pop into Romano's kitchen. "Hey, Romano, how are you?"

He came forward wearing a smile. "Hi, my darling Rosebud. Is it time for your shift already? I can't believe time has slipped away from me like it has today."

Curious, I asked, "What have you been up to?" As I looked around, I could see piles of paper spread out on the prep table.

"Just going through some of my recipes trying to find my favorite one for Hungarian goulash. I wanted to try it again sometime this weekend."

We had a quick coffee together before I had to run off for my shift. Fortunately, it was quiet and seemed to be a normal day, with clients coming and going. Most of them were regulars. Mimi was not around, probably because she'd been working the night shift, and so I was alone most of the time. When Bambi came to take over while I went on break, I went into the kitchen and ended up sitting alone at the prep table nibbling on a tuna sandwich Romano had whipped up for me. He remained busy with the supper crowd, which always clamored for his chicken supreme. At the end of my break, he broke away just long enough to blow me a kiss as I was leaving.

At the end of my shift, Mimi came to collect my receipts, and I was glad to see her. She'd be back soon, and I couldn't wait to get home, for I was really tired and more than ready for a night of undisturbed sleep. However, I wasn't certain how soon that was going to happen, since Steve never showed up to take me home. I tried reaching him by phone. No answer.

I called Brian and then Mike. Neither answered. What is it with them? I simply left a message with each of them, telling them what was going on but not to worry because I would call a cab and head home. I didn't want to use PUP because I didn't want them to know where I lived. I ended my voice mail message to both with "Just let me know what's going on, because I'm beginning to worry about Steve."

Mimi had come back to the front to take over for me. I'd already gotten my purse and was still waiting for the cab to come when Mimi asked, "No Mike tonight?"

"No, not tonight," I said.

Mimi looked at me and asked, "Is everything all right?"

"It will be as soon as I get some sleep. How about you? Is it hard to switch to nighttime working hours?"

"To be honest, I don't know how Cindy does it. I can't wait for her to return to work," she said with a laugh.

The cab arrived and honked its horn for me to come out, which annoyed me, but I was too tired to put up a fuss. I said goodnight to Mimi and got into the cab.

CHAPTER 31

When the cabbie pulled into my development, I was glad to see the regular person in the guardhouse. I asked, "Anything going on, Bill?"

"Naw, it's been quiet. Have a good night, Ms. Bennett."

Taking no chances, I had the cab drop me off two doors down from my house so he wouldn't know where I lived. After he left, I walked quickly to my house, glad to be home after a long day. I put in the code for the garage door opener and rushed inside, anxious to be safely home. As I entered, I called out, "Sweet Pea, I'm home."

I heard not a peep from her. This sometimes happened if she was upset with me when I've left her for a long time, and then she wants me to come to her, so I put down my purse and went through the house to her favorite spot in the living room. No Sweet Pea. Just then I heard a gravelly voice behind me, which made my heart sink. "Welcome home, Rosalie." Chills ran up and down my body, for I knew who it was.

There she stood, disheveled, looking like a mad woman. Her eyes were wild and bulging, her hair greasy and matted, her clothes dirty and wrinkled. Her face became contorted with rage when she saw me, and I became frantic. "Where's Sweet Pea? What did you do with her, Mama?"

"Ha, wouldn't you like to know?" she snarled, enjoying my worry.

I took a step toward her, ready to grab her. She quickly spit out, "I put her in the closet."

Sweet Pea had an odd habit. If you put her in a room and closed the door, she wouldn't bark or do anything; she'd just sit there. Now even more upset, I looked toward the front hall closet and then turned back to Mama. "If you hurt her in any way …"

"She's fine," she insisted with annoyance. She waved her hand at me in dismissal but blocked me from the front entrance and Sweet Pea.

"Just what it is you want, Mama? Why are you here?" I demanded, hands fisted at my side.

"If you had just left things alone, there wouldn't have been an issue. I'm *not* going to be the only one to take the fall for the little girls, you're going down with me. This is all your doing, Rosalie—or should I call you Rosebud? Oh, yes, I know all about your little nickname. Very cute."

"Where did you go so wrong, Mama? Since when do you think it is okay to use little girls for men's pleasure?" I had a quick vision and asked, "Is that what happened to you when you were little?"

The look that came across her face, filled with such anguish and sorrow, took my breath away. Mama, obviously distraught, just stared at me and didn't stay a word. I took advantage of her pause to ask, "Isn't it B.B. you should be angry with? He's the one who is selling you out. You must realize that, don't you?"

Just then my cell phone rang, making both of us jump. I reached for it, and Mama screamed, "Don't touch that."

I continued to pull it from my purse and said, "If I don't answer it, whoever it is will keep calling until I do. You don't want that, do you?"

"I said don't answer it. Give me your phone right now." She lunged at me and grabbed it out of my hands, knocking me back and off balance. I grabbed the end table and righted myself.

As she read what showed, she asked, "It says it's Ron. Who's that?"

"Nobody I know, must be a sales call," I answered, nervously.

"Oh, c'mon. I know better than that." She stepped toward me in a threatening way.

"Oh, all right, he's an old boyfriend who won't leave me alone. Just let the call go, and don't answer it," I said, knowing Ron would be able to see I was home and would wonder why I didn't answer. Surprising Mama, I stepped forward and yanked the phone from her hand, clasping it tightly in mine. She just smiled in a weird way and obviously liked our tussling, which made me fear what might come if I continued to confront her.

It became her turn as she sprang forward and pushed me back, making me stumble. "Sit down right there," she ordered, pointing to one of the two chairs on either side of the fireplace. As I turned to settle myself into the chair, I switched on the recorder on the phone and placed it next to me. She never noticed anything, for she was deep in thought and wore a sick smile. "So you're already cheating on your boyfriend, is that it? You're just a slut like all the girls at the lounge. My god, what is the matter with all of you that you can't be satisfied with the man you already have and have to go after someone else's? You're just whores, all of you."

"Who are you talking about?" I demanded, hoping I could keep her talking.

She became infuriated, and her face turned all funny. "That whore Melissa. Who did she think she was anyway? He wouldn't have been interested in her if she hadn't thrown herself at him."

I didn't dare say anything, though I was thinking of her dead husband, David Masterly, and Melissa together, yet I didn't really believe he was B.B. What was really going on? Something wasn't making sense, so I prodded her, "Do you mean Sally?" I asked, hoping to get some information about her murder.

"No, not her," she answered, apparently disgusted that I'd even asked. "She wouldn't have hurt a flea, but they didn't care and said she'd have to go anyway."

"Did B.B. say that?" I asked, wanting to know if he was responsible for Sally's death.

Just then, there was furious knocking on the front door, which caused Sweet Pea to start barking. Her high, shrill barking and the loud knocking at the door made Mama reach for her head with both hands. "Shut up, all of you," she screamed as she pulled out a Glock from the folds of her skirt and shakily aimed it at me.

"Just settle down, Mama. I'll make the noise stop," I said to sooth her, "Just let me get the door."

"I know exactly what you're doing," she exclaimed. "Do you think I'm stupid? *I'll* get the door—you stay right there."

I watched her sidle to the front door while she kept her gun trained on me. She hollered through the door, "Who's there?"

"It's Ron, Rosalie."

"Ah, the boyfriend returns. Let's let him in so I can see how you're going to handle this one, shall we?"

"No, Mama, just tell him to go away," I urged, panic rising as I realized what he'd be getting into. She flashed a wicked smile my way. My saying no was all she'd needed to prompt her to let him in.

She opened the door wide. I heard Ron gasp when he saw her and the gun. "C'mon in, lover boy, don't just stand there."

"Where's Rosalie? Have you hurt her?" he asked as he came forward.

"Not yet, but you can watch me do that if you'd like, or are you here to save the day?" she asked with a smug smile as she continued to nudge him forward, the gun against his back.

When Ron entered the living room, he was white as a sheet but wore a tight smile of relief when he saw me sitting in the chair, untouched. "Oh, my dear Rosalie, are you okay?"

"I'm so sorry, Ron, for getting you involved like this," I said as my eyes filled.

Ron leaned down and patted my head. "Don't you worry, honey," he whispered. "I've already called the police."

He blocked my view from Mama so I held my finger to my lips to quiet him. "Shhh. Don't say a word about that, okay?"

"What are you two talking about? I can hear you whispering," Mama demanded.

Ron stood up straight, making him seem taller than his 5'7", and he immediately spoke up, "I'm just telling Rosie not to worry. I'm here now."

"How sweet is that? Right, Rosebud?"

I nodded my head, not knowing where she was headed. "Hey, lover boy, pull over one of those chairs in the kitchen and place it right next to Rosebud there. That way, I can watch the two of you at the same time."

Ron followed her orders and sat next to me. Mama watched us with interest and then said, "You know, Rosebud, maybe you did the right thing by dumping Ron. You two sure don't look like lovers. I sure as hell can't picture the two of you in bed together either. You don't match up. You're taller than he is, aren't you? That ought to make things interesting."

I could feel Ron tense up as he heard what Mama was saying. I couldn't imagine he'd ever been accused of being anyone's lover before, and I knew he must be mortified by the thought. Although Ron is a nice man, not many would consider him good-looking or even a great catch at first glance, but he's the type of man who grows on you. By now, I was sure he was curious about why she thought we'd been lovers. I patted his hand, hoping it would calm him, and at first, he tried to pull it away, embarrassed, then he grabbed and squeezed my hand. We smiled at each other weakly as he mouthed, "Rosebud?"

"So how come you're here, Ron? Wanting to get a little honey, are you?"

I could feel Ron hesitate, not knowing what she meant or how to respond, then he blurted, "Sure, why not, right?" trying to play the game. He looked at me, wondering whether that had been the right response, and then he glared at Mama. If looks could kill.

"You men are all alike, always wanting your honey, no matter what. You men make me sick." she screamed. She began to wave the gun around, and it looked as though she wasn't sure of what to do next. It was obvious she hadn't had much sleep since she'd gone into hiding, and it was showing as she began to unravel. She was acting crazy, which really scared me.

"So what do you think, Ron, of your girlfriend here who's always putting her nose into where it doesn't belong? Did you get sick of her doing that too?"

Ron just sat there without responding, which angered her, so she yelled, "Well, did you?"

Ron looked at me and hesitantly replied, "Sometimes."

In spite of being nervous about Mama's erratic behavior, I swallowed a smile at Ron's brave response. Poor man. I knew he was out of his league dealing with Mama because his wife, Irene, was timid and good-natured, very much the opposite of Mama.

"Here she is at the Purple Passion Lounge telling *me* what I can and cannot do in my own place. She thinks that selling little girls is wrong, while every day she works at the lounge she's doing just that, only with girls who are older. What do you think about that? Is that the kind of girlfriend you want, someone who thinks what *you're* doing is wrong but it's all right for *her* to do the same?"

Ron avoided my eyes when I turned to him, and I knew he was taken aback more than a bit. His face turned beet red, for I'm sure he hadn't been aware of what I had been doing at the lounge. Neither my job at the lounge nor what I was trying to accomplish working there was anything he'd ever approve of, as much as he might care for me. I felt my face flush as red as his, as I was mortified by what was happening, and I hated the idea that Ron might think I lacked good morals and ethics. In addition, it hurt to listen to what Mama said about me.

As Ron remained quiet, sitting upright in his seat, Mama stated, "You're lucky to be rid of her, she's not worth it. Should I just kill her now, lover boy, and get it over with?" she asked, laughing hysterically

Ron stirred in his seat and shook his head. "Please don't do that," he urged in a small, terrified voice.

Mama moved forward, stood over Ron, and pointed the gun at his head. "Well, Rosebud, want me to get rid of him for you once and for all? One of you has to go. Who will it be?"

"Ron's not your problem, and you know it," I said in a firm voice. When she hesitated, I continued, "Don't you get it? No one stepped in to help you after the raid, did they? Not Tony. Not Johnny. Not B.B. They're the ones who've left you hanging out to dry. It's B.B. you should go after, Mama—he's the one."

She turned her full attention on me, "What do you know about B.B., anyway? Are you after him too?" she asked, outraged. She stepped toward me and pointed the gun at me. "He belongs to me, not you or anyone else. He's *my* baby brother, not yours."

What was it Romano had said about Mama as a young girl? I recalled now he said she had a brother. Good lord. B.B. was her baby brother? All of a sudden, everything was beginning to make sense.

That is when we heard the sirens coming our way.

"What's that?" asked Mama with alarm. "Did you call the cops?" she asked, looking from one of us to the other. Before we could answer, the front door was pushed open and my enemy the chief of police was striding toward us. When he saw Mama, he ordered, "Put down your gun,

Mama. No need for this. Just come quietly and there'll be no fuss."

"Oh no, you don't, baby brother, you're not taking *me* in. You need to take in Rosebud here."

She had to be kidding.—the chief of police was her baby brother, B.B.? I knew I was in big trouble when I saw B.B.'s backup through the door—the two goons, who had questioned me in Mimi's office. I needed to do something, but what? Suddenly, instinctively, I yelled, "Good for you, Mama, stick to your guns—don't let them take you in. B.B. isn't here to protect you, he's here to take you in so it will be you who takes the fall for everyone else."

"Shut up, bitch." B.B. said as he pulled out his gun and aimed it at me.

"Stand firm, Mama." I encouraged her, and she straightened up and raised her chin a bit.

In a stronger voice, she said, "Franklin, you've got to protect me. I was just following your orders ..."

"Be quiet, Mama, and don't say another word, hear me?"

"I'm your sister, for God's sake, and I'm not going to be the one to go to jail."

"Just shut up, Mama, I mean it."

It was fascinating to watch the various expressions cross Mama's face as she realized her brother was not there to save her. Then she purposefully turned her gun away from me toward B.B. When the shot rang out, B.B. looked down in disbelief at the blood spreading across his chest. At the same time, Mama looked stunned when she realized she was the one responsible for what was happening to him.

I saw Mike coming through the door with his gun drawn and ready just as Mama spotted him. She raised her gun and took aim, and just as B.B. hit the floor, two shots rang out. I watched in terror as both Mike and Mama fell to the floor.

I jumped from my chair and raced to Mike, who was lying on the floor and groaning. When he saw me hovering over him, he gave me a crooked smile and said, "Damn, this hurts."

I yelled to Ron, "Call 911, and hurry."

We could see Mama couldn't harm us, for she was flat on her back, not moving. After Ron made the 911 call, he went over to Mama and kicked at her body to make sure she was dead. "She's got a bullet hole between her eyes. She's a goner," he yelled.

I was holding Mike tight in my arms, murmuring "Thank you, Mike. Thank you dear, sweet Mike for saving our lives." When Ron approached, Mike stirred and said, "Out front. Two jerks out front."

Ron picked up Mike's gun and shakily headed out the door. There were the two cops, who had come with B.B., spread-eagled on the ground, still unconscious from when Mike had knocked them out.

The ambulance and Brian arrived at the same time. He took one look at Mike in my arms and at the expression on my face and raised his eyebrows. Then he heard scratching in the front-hall closet and asked, "What's going on?" He opened it to find Sweet Pea looking exhausted and worried, so he scooped her up into his arms and soothed her. "Rosie, you go ahead and ride in the ambulance with Mike; I'll take care of her."

As the EMTs lifted the gurney into the ambulance, and as a special allowance, I climbed into the back with Mike. I could see reporters arriving, and I watched as Brian readied himself for them. He continued to hold Sweet Pea, who, for once, wasn't wriggling and was just glad to be safe in his arms. He talked to Ron, probably advising him on what to say and not say to the reporters, since it was still a continuing investigation. I could see Mike was right that Brian always drew attention, for all the female reporters gathered around him and left Ron standing by himself. I could hear them exclaiming over Sweet Pea while ogling Brian. How was this all going to end?

CHAPTER 32

A lthough it was very painful, it turned out Mike's injury wasn't serious. Mama's shot had gone clear through his shoulder and skimmed a nerve, which was going to take a few weeks to heal completely.

Ron had seen Mama enter my house when he was watching the camera trained on it. As a good neighbor, and because he'd seen someone around my house earlier, he'd called the police. When he saw movement in my house, he'd called me, but when I didn't answer the phone, he knew I was in trouble and had come over.

He would never look at me the same way again, for what Mama had said about my role at the Purple Passion Lounge had stuck with him. Even after he was told why I was at the lounge and what my real role was, he treated me differently—in some ways, with more respect. His whole involvement and experience with the incident caused him to stand straighter and gave him a swagger, which made him more appealing. When we met outside a few days later, I noticed his wife admiring him behind his back, which made me smile.

Poor Steve. After Tony and Johnny discussed grabbing Mike for ransom, they sent Lorenzo to chase down the car that dropped me off. Not being the sharpest knife in the drawer as Mimi described Lorenzo, he had mugged Steve thinking he was Mike. Once again, Steve was rescued and had a lump on his head, much like the time before at Lowes. Brian laughingly told me Steve asked never again to be assigned to watch me.

Mike and Brian had staked out Brian's boss's house and had found pay dirt or, as they said, dirty pay. He was indeed very involved in human trafficking and held sex orgies with several public people, who now were scrambling to come up with top-notch lawyers to defend them. Because Brian and Mike had been working with the FBI and brought them in for the raid, most of those tangled up in this would get some jail time and hefty fines.

In addition, Brian found out that the diamond ring we had found tucked away in Melissa's things had indeed been purchased by the chief of police. I didn't believe she'd been in love with him, for he was not a very lovable man. I felt her wanting to escape from that relationship had been the impetus for her desire to escape Las Vegas.

Unbelievably, Tony and Johnny walked away with just fines for allowing the Purple Passion Lounge to use sordid business practices and not doing due diligence about what was going on under their noses. They threw all the blame onto Mama and B.B. and said they'd been the ones responsible for the deaths of both Melissa and Sally, among other things. They confirmed the chief of police had been crazy about Melissa, and they said that although they couldn't be sure, they believed it was Mama who had her killed. They also said they believed B.B. had killed Sally in retaliation for Mama's murdering Melissa. It was a wild tumbleweed of destruction.

It seemed that the chief of police's involvement in everything would lead to a much wider investigation of all the things that happened during his reign, which gave me an opening to bring out the facts about Jeff. I didn't care how it came about just as long as Jeff's name was cleared. When I heard his case would be quietly reopened, I assumed that meant when the truth came out, there'd be an article tucked away in the newspaper naming the chief of police as responsible for Jeff's murder. I think that it'd probably end up for B.B. as it had for Mama and even Jeff, himself; it was the chief's turn to take the fall for everything.

Days later, Brian came by to check on Mike. We sat at the kitchen table having coffee while Sweet Pea lay at Brian's feet, content to have him near her as he shared some time with us. We laughed at Brian's obvious delight at taking down the station manager, who had given him so much trouble. He, of course, had been assigned to the lead story and was able to portray himself as the station's top reporter, making us smile. Brian quipped, "Maybe when I tire of all this investigative stuff, news reporting can be my new career."

Mike and I looked at each other and in unison said, "Don't give up your day job just yet."

Brian looked us, shook his head, patted Sweet Pea, and turned to leave. "See you two later."

After Brian left, I went back to the coded notes, curious about what they said, for I'd ignored my intuition and hadn't bothered with them after I found out they wouldn't have been allowed as evidence. As I reviewed the pages and the two anagrams I hadn't been able to decipher, there they were—robbery bath meant baby brother and heartb meant Bertha, known as Mama. I hoped I wouldn't be so quick to dismiss my intuition next time.

I sat at my desk and ruminated about the Purple Passion Lounge, which had been closed for the previous two weeks by then. I was due to meet Mimi there that afternoon, and I was curious to learn what she wanted and what she intended to do with the lounge.

"Hey, Rosie, what're you up to?" Mike asked, leaning into my office from the doorway. He'd stayed at the house for the past few weeks to allow his wound to heal and to act as my guard to make sure there was no other fallout from the entire incident. He and Brian wanted me safe, and I was grateful for that.

Since the shooting, Mike hadn't been his usual self. He continued to be a bit standoffish, as he'd been the few days before the shooting. He was acting strange around me, and I wondered whether his pain was causing him to act that way. I decided to leave him be and give him space to heal.

"Nothing much," I answered. "Just wondering what Mimi has to say. I can't believe she'd reopen the lounge, but I guess I'll find out soon enough."

"And if she does ... will you go back?" asked Mike, worry in his voice.

I looked at him, and my heart fluttered. He was as handsome as ever, with his dark hair curling now that it was longer. His dark eyes were serious as he waited for my response. "No. I don't ever want to be involved in anything like that again." Shivers ran up and down my body, warning me I might not have a choice, but I shook off the feeling and turned to him with a smile.

Death at the Lake

"Good choice, Rosie." He came to where I was sitting and stood behind me and leaned down closer. "Want me to drive you in?" he asked in a soft voice.

"No, thanks, I'll drive myself. That'll give you time to get some of your things together and pack for your trip," I answered, despondently. The mystery man had given Brian and Mike time to get themselves squared away before they moved on to help him with something new he wanted them to investigate in Boston.

My heart flopped when I realized how much I would miss working with them and seeing them every day. It would be strange not to have them around, leaving me alone; Sweet Pea would be desolate without their attention. I was beginning to feel like a sailboat without a rudder. Time to move on, I thought, with little enthusiasm as I got up. Time to meet with Mimi.

I drove to the Purple Passion Lounge. When I arrived, it looked unfamiliar without any parked cars and a valet to greet me. I found the front door unlocked, and there was a note telling me to lock up after me. I stepped into the front area, where I had spent so much time, and I shivered, recalling all that happened while I'd been working there. So much violence.

I headed down the hallway and heard voices and laughter coming from Romano's kitchen. When I peeked in, I was ecstatic to see Romano sitting at the prep table with Mimi, and both looked up at me with big smiles, pleased to see me. Romano jumped up from the table and hugged me tightly before releasing me and giving me loud smacks on each cheek. "Oh, my darling Rosebud, I'm so glad to see you."

Mimi said, "Rosalie, thank you for coming." She patted the seat next to her. "I know you two must be wondering why I've invited you here, so let me begin."

Romano pushed a freshly poured cup of mint tea and a plate of homemade cookies toward me. I reached for a cookie to nibble on to hide the discomfort I was feeling.

"Rosalie, more than any of us, you are responsible for straightening out all the sordid goings-on around here, and I want to personally thank you for that. There aren't many who would have done so much and endured what you've gone through."

My cheeks turned pink; I was embarrassed. I didn't know what to say, for what she said was probably true, but had I really had a choice?

"You asked me before if I knew what I was going to do about the lounge and whether I was going to sell it."

"Yes, I did. I'm very curious to learn what you've decided."

"Good, because it involves you too."

My eyebrows shot up. "What do you mean?"

"Here's what I'm planning. See what you two think. The Purple Passion Lounge can't continue the way it is—we can all agree on that, right? What I'm proposing is to tear this place down and rebuild it as a small, fancy restaurant—a fine dining restaurant with fabulous musical entertainment. It's a valuable piece of property in a great location, and with the right people in charge, I think it can be very successful, don't you agree, Romano?"

Obviously, this was news to him too. "Probably so. With the right people, of course."

Mimi and I chuckled. "Of course," Mimi said, and that's where you come in, Romano. I'd like it to become your restaurant. I would be responsible for the expense of rebuilding. But we'd be joint owners. However, if you get it up and running successfully, it could become yours alone after five years in return for a modest down payment for legal purposes. Since I own the land, you'd make normal lease payments to me for use of the land, plus a small amount toward repayment for the reconstruction of the structure, which would put pressure on both of us to make it work. It makes sense doesn't it?"

I could see Romano grappling with the idea and becoming excited about the possibilities. I wondered how I would fit into all of this, for I had no desire to run a restaurant.

"Of course," Mimi continued, "I have my lawyers working on that now, so you can have your own lawyer review it to make any changes you want if we both can agree on them. I don't expect they'll be anything we can't work out."

"How exciting, Romano, I'm so happy for you." I said.

"And now you, Rosalie. Here's what I propose for you. I'd like to use the other half of the property for the nonprofit organization you worked with to protect the little girls. I understand their lease is coming up and they're going to be looking for another place to operate. I know you're interested in stopping human trafficking, and if you're willing, I would like to hire you to work with them to make it happen. You'd be responsible for meeting with the architects to design a suitable building and to make sure to stay within the budget. Of course, we'd be in contact with each other all along the way."

"Oh, Mimi, of course, I'd love to do that." Tears came to my eyes as happened every time I thought of the little girls, especially Isabella.

The three of us talked for hours and went over more details while Romano poured us Champagne to toast our comradery and venture. Each of us was excited for our own reasons. Things were looking up … at least for the moment.

CHAPTER 33

When I arrived home, I was surprised to see that Mike and Brian were there, and anxious to hear what Mimi had to say. After I told them what had happened, Brian pulled out the Champagne he'd brought with him to celebrate our last night together, and now my exciting news.

Cindy called to see what was going on and to say goodbye to Brian and Mike. She was out of town, spending time renewing and growing her relationship with her former boyfriend, who was back in her life. Their relationship was getting serious, and none of us knew whether she'd want to get back into the investigating business with Brian and Mike.

After many toasts, we ended up going around the corner to Sam's Roadhouse for pizza and drinks before calling it a night. I was proud of myself because I didn't make a fool of myself when we talked about Brian and Mike's leaving in the morning. I didn't want to embarrass them or myself, so we kept up light chatter until we were ready to end the night.

Back at the house, Mike and Brian sat at the kitchen table while they talked about what they'd need to do to complete their part of the investigation with the FBI, which they'd be able to do in Boston once there. While they were talking, I picked up Sweet Pea, stepped forward, gave each of them a light kiss on the cheek, and bid them goodnight.

"Goodnight, my queen and her princess," said Mike in a soft voice. I turned and looked at him without saying a word. Brian looked at us and was silent. What could I say when I was so choked up with emotion that I wouldn't be able to force out any words?

The next morning, I grabbed the covers and tossed them over my head, trying to avoid the beginning of the day, for I knew what was coming. The day marched forward anyway, and soon I could smell coffee brewing. As I was about to jump out of bed to make my way downstairs, I heard Mike coming upstairs. He knocked on the door. "Good morning, Rosie, I have a cup of coffee for you. Want me to bring it in?

I sat up in bed and decided it was the perfect thing for that moment. "Yes, please."

After Mike handed me the coffee, he sat on the edge of the bed. Sweet Pea was delighted to have him there and nudged him to make room for her beside him. He chuckled.

"Here, hold this a minute, please," I said as I handed him my cup. I moved to the middle of the bed and patted the empty space next to me to give him more space to sit.

He smiled and handed back my coffee, and then he moved closer on the bed. "Rosie, we need to talk," he said in a serious voice.

Panic rumbled in my stomach. "Okay. What's this about?"

"Well, I suppose it's about me," he said uneasily, suddenly shy. "I hardly know where to begin, actually."

"How about the beginning?" I teased.

He reached toward me, cupping my cheek in his hand as his eyes burned into mine, melting me in their warmth. "Ah, the beginning … When I first met you, you looked so young and innocent. I was crazy about you from the first moment I saw you, and it's grown to be so much more for me than that."

"What are you talking about, Mike?" I asked, my heart pounding.

"I want you to know how difficult it's been to be here under your roof and not do something about it, but as long as I was on duty here as your guard, I couldn't."

Seeing my surprise, he stopped and didn't say another word. We just stared at each other. Was he saying what I thought he was? Is that why he'd been acting so funny, so standoffish, lately? I sat frozen, unable to say anything because I couldn't find the words to express my feelings for him.

Misunderstanding my silence, Mike rose from the bed and said, "Sorry, I guess I'm out of line."

As he turned away to leave, I held out my hand and said, "Wait."

He hesitated, then blurted out, "I think you must realize I'm in love with you. I thought you had feelings for me too, but maybe this isn't the time nor place."

My heart was beating so fast I couldn't catch my breath. Where had this come from, when had this happened? I cried out, "But ..."

He'd already left the room. I was confused. Although there was no doubt I had deep feelings for Mike, I'd been afraid to let them come to the foreground because there was a part of me that was terrified of getting involved. Sometimes, when a friendship turned into a more serious relationship, it could ruin a relationship of any kind, and I didn't want to lose what I had with Mike—or even Brian. Was I willing to take a chance with Mike?

As I lay in bed, I considered my relationship with Jeff. I now realized I had been very naïve and much too involved in all the things that didn't really matter, all the fluff. I'd been wrapped up in how the wedding was going to look to others and, as a psychic, I had ignored my responsibility to act upon what had been shown to me. Yes, you had been warned, I chided myself.

And as naïve as I was at that time, Jeff was too. He was not only young but also lacked life experience, which had been evident in the way he'd handled his awareness of the drug dealing at his precinct. That relationship and what Mike and I could have were like night and day, because Mike was older and had seen and experienced life in many different ways. It was enticing to think of allowing Mike further into my life in a new way, yet, was he right for me? Were the time and the place right?

I hurriedly dressed and dashed downstairs to call out, "Mike?"

He turned to me as I raced into his arms, and they tightened around me as I professed breathlessly, "I think this is definitely the time and place for us, Mike."

He leaned down and kissed me fully on the lips, making me weak with desire. He murmured, "I love you, Rosie."

"I love you too, Mike," I said, knowing how right those words were.

A few minutes later, we had to pull away from one another when Brian arrived to pick up Mike and drive to the airport. I was sad to say goodbye to the two most important men in my life, and although I'd been determined not to allow myself to become emotional, my restraint went out the window and I cried when we said our goodbyes. As Brian headed out the door, Mike and I held onto each other for a bit longer. We searched each other's eyes, knowing they shone with love for one another. "Just return to me safe and sound, that's all I ask," I pleaded.

"God willing," he whispered into my ear, leaving me with a hole in my stomach, for that was no promise. One last kiss, and they were gone. That was it. Nothing more.

I went upstairs to make my bed and instead lay down, feeling lost, so I closed my eyes and fell asleep with Sweet Pea next to me. Much later, I stirred when my cell phone rang. I'd almost decided not to answer it when I suddenly felt I should. "Hello?" I croaked.

"Rosie? This is Jacklyn from the agency. We have a special request. We have found some of Isabella's relatives in Santa Fe, New Mexico. They can't afford to come here to pick her up, and she refuses to go there unless you are with her. Our job is to reunite her with her relatives to provide her with a family of her own people. This is a little bit unorthodox, but would you be willing to take her to Santa Fe to meet her relatives?"

I was stunned, and my thoughts flew. I didn't have a good feeling about what was waiting for her there, but I surely didn't want Isabella to go without someone to protect her. With Mike and Brian no longer in Las Vegas and not much else going on, I certainly had the time to spare. "Yes," I answered, "I'm willing to do that, with one condition. If I find that isn't a good situation for her, I want to be able to bring her back."

"Well, I'm not sure about that. We've never had that happen, so I guess we'll have to cross that bridge when we come to it."

"That's a deal. When can I pick her up?"

"Anytime, really. It's up to you."

"Please tell her I'm on my way."

I turned to Sweet Pea, who was watching me with interest. I leaned down and gathered her into my arms. "Want to go to Santa Fe with Isabella and me?"

CHECK OUT THE NEXT BOOK IN
THE DEATH CARD SERIES

DEATH
RETURNS

Book 3

The Death Card Series

By

J.S. Peck

BEJEWELED PUBLISHING
LAS VEGAS, NEVADA

CHAPTER 1

N ow, what had I gotten myself into? What had I agreed to do? Was I making a mistake? I closed my eyes and replayed the conversation in my head.

"Rosie? This is Jacklyn from the agency. We have a special request. We have found some of Isabella's relatives in Santa Fe, New Mexico. They can't afford to come here to pick her up, and she refuses to go there unless you are with her. Our job is to reunite her with her relatives to provide her a family of her own people. This is a little bit unorthodox, but would you be willing to take her to Santa Fe to meet her relatives?"

Isabella, just 11 years old, was the oldest of the four little girls who were set to be auctioned off at the Purple Passion Lounge as part of their human trafficking scheme. She became attached to me when I helped them escape, and had now taken to calling me Mama because she wanted me to be her new mother. However, that was not going to happen for all sorts of reasons, which she had a hard time understanding.

I had agreed to what they'd asked ... with one condition. If I found that Santa Fe was not a good situation for Isabella, I wanted to be able to bring her back to Las Vegas. Since her own parents had refused to take her back, I wasn't about to simply leave her defenseless with a bunch of strangers, and Jacklyn and I'd agreed we'd cross that bridge if and when we came to it. The bigger problem was that, as an intuitive, I didn't feel good about anything we were headed to.

I felt Isabella's hand on my arm. For the past few days while we readied for our trip, Isabella had been tugging on my sleeve every two minutes, saying something to me that she'd learned new in English. Ever since we'd been together last, she'd been furiously studying the English language and driving the woman at the safe house crazy. I was getting a little taste of that already. The surprising thing was Isabella's English was exceptionally good. She seemed to be a natural linguist.

"Mama? Can I wear my new dress on the airplane or should I wait until I get to Santa Fe?"

"What do you want to do?"

"I want to wear it as soon as possible!"

I laughed for she was a girl after my own heart. What was the point of delaying the pleasure of wearing something new? We'd spent a full two days of preparation to get ready for our trip by shopping and then packing our new clothes in matching suitcases. My silky pup, Sweet Pea, was coming with us, so I wouldn't be worried about her being at a dog sitter's. My neighbor was going to watch over my house and water the plants, so all would be in good order when I returned. We were ready to go!

Now, as I looked around, I had to smile for I didn't know who was more excited about going to Santa Fe— Isabella, me or my dog! As we stood at the airport waiting for our flight, Isabella asked with excitement, "When is our plane arriving?"

I could feel eyes on us. I was aware that we probably looked like a motley threesome. Isabella, even at the age of 11, turned heads with her Mexican beauty—light coffee skin; dark, silky hair; and shining black eyes over a smile as wide as her face. She was so petite that when she held Sweet Pea in her arms, I could barely see her behind the dog.

I, on the other hand, probably looked like the nervous wreck I was with my uncontrollable, long hair flying around my face, which now creased with worry. I hadn't been able to reach Mike, the new love in my life, to tell him of my sudden change in plans, and I was frustrated to realize how many times I'd tried to reach him to no avail. Of course, that was part of his being on assignment – not always available when I'd like. Now that Mike and I were developing our relationship in a more romantic way, I knew he'd worry if he discovered I'd left Las Vegas without his knowing where I was. Ever since we'd done investigative work together, both Mike and his partner, Brian, had become very protective of me, and although I didn't feel I needed their protection, it was easier to just let them know what was happening.

I felt someone at my elbow and looked to see a rather large woman pointing at Isabella. "Are you her mother?" the woman asked. I said "No" at the same time Isabella said "Yes." The woman looked confused. "Yes," I amended, not wanting to get into a public disagreement with Isabella. "Why?"

"Mexicans and dogs aren't allowed on the airplane."

I was floored, and looked at her in disbelief. Who said that type of things in today's age?

"Ah, there you are, Mabel," a voice behind me said with relief. After he took a look at my face, he added, "Oh, no. What did she say?"

"Something very rude, I'm afraid."

"I'm so sorry, but please don't mind her. She has Alzheimer's and moments of saying the most bizarre things. I hope she hasn't offended you."

"Just my daughter and my dog," I said with annoyance. I looked at Isabella who wore such a pleased expression on her face that I was puzzled. I reached out and patted the man's arm. "It's okay, really. I know you have your hands full."

"Thanks for understanding. C'mon Mabel, they're calling our flight." They headed toward their gate and I watched them go with sympathy for what they were going through.

I turned to Isabella, who was grinning from ear to ear. "What?" I asked.

"You told that man I was your daughter, Mama."

"No, I didn't, honey."

"Yes, you did. You said, 'Just my daughter and my dog.'"

I thought about what she'd said and realized I'd said exactly that without thinking. "Oh my, Isabella, I guess I did." I gave her a hug and whispered, "But you know that's not true. You know we're here together so I can take you to Santa Fe to meet your family, right?"

"I know," she said sadly, lowering her head.

As I turned away from her, my huge Dooney & Bourke traveling purse fell off my shoulder, and landed with a thud, scattering some of its contents. My tarot cards spilled and there it was the—Death card popping up on top, staring me in the face—a sign for me that there was going to be an upcoming murder, or death, of someone I knew, or would soon meet.

"Give it a rest," I mumbled. Still, the card sat there waiting for me to pick it up, and again, there was that feeling that Santa Fe held more in store for us than simply meeting Isabella's family. With a sigh, I collected and stuffed everything back in my bag. I could hear our flight being called, so we loaded Sweet Pea in her carrier and boarded with the others travelling first class.

Once in the plane, I explained to Isabella we were going to be landing in Albuquerque, New Mexico, where we'd spend the night, and then we'd rent a car the next morning and drive the hour or so north to Santa Fe. "Oh, Mama, I'm so excited! I've never been in an airplane before!" I decided not to scold for her calling me Mama. It would be a waste of time, anyhow, because ever since I'd rescued her that was her name for me.

I smiled at her enthusiasm. My own enjoyment for flying had come to an end a long time ago when the seats on planes became smaller, and I'd find myself thigh to thigh with a complete stranger. Since the dress code had become less strict, flying to me was more like riding a bus in the sky, and much less exciting than it had been.

"Mama, am I going to see Indians in Santa Fe? Real live Indians?"

"Yes, Isabella, I bet you will. Here, let's Google all about them on my iPhone and see what we can find out."

Isabella looked at me with stars in her eyes. "Okay!"

I did my magic, and she hung on my shoulder as I read to her aloud, "Of the 19 Native American communities in New Mexico, eight are near Santa Fe. All eight are Pueblo

Indian tribes and their communities are referred to as pueblos.

"Many of these pueblos, such as the Taos Pueblo which is thought to have been continuously occupied for close to 1,000 years, were established centuries ago. Each pueblo has its own tribal government, traditions, and ceremonies, and is a sovereign and separate entity. The pueblos typically welcome visitors and much can be learned about Native American culture by visiting the pueblos, especially during the specific dances and feast days open to the public."

"Can we visit a pueblo, Mama?"

"I think that's a great idea," I answered, pleased by her curiosity; yet, I became disturbed by a sudden fear that washed over me. I had a vision of me standing on a cliff, calling out for Isabella. Goosebumps ran up and down my body and made me shiver, making me wonder what we were getting ourselves into.

It was a short flight and before I knew it, we were wheels down, ready to land in Albuquerque. It's a beautiful city and hostess to magnificent and successful hot air balloon festivals each fall. By the time we'd let Sweet Pea out to go to the bathroom, and we'd loaded the car I'd rented, we all were dragging, the day was ending, and we were getting hungry. We headed to the Hyatt Place Albuquerque Airport Hotel and settled in our room because it was too late to wander around the city, so we were content to order room service, including Sweet Pea's dinner.

"Oh, Mama, this room is so pretty. Look outside and see all the lights."

It tickled me to watch Isabella run and jump on the bed with Sweet Pea, but they immediately hopped off as soon as they heard the knock on the door announcing our food was there. Isabella's eyes got as big as saucers as she watched the server roll in the tray loaded with plates covered in silver to keep the food warm. She became entranced by the idea of someone in a uniform pulling out her chair and serving her. I had to smile at how much she liked it, and I was sure she'd want more of this kind of attention in the future.

After dinner, we took Sweet Pea for a final walk of the day. When we returned, I readied Isabella for bed and tucked her in the queen bed closest to the bathroom with Sweet Pea snuggled next to her. I picked up the local newspaper to read in silence while Isabella nodded off.

The weather report said it should be beautiful—not too hot, not too cold. Good, I thought, for once, I've packed the right things to wear. As I looked through the pages of the newspaper, I saw an article about a murder in Santa Fe. When I read the story, I felt goosebumps cross my entire body, making me uncomfortable. I felt this murder was somehow tied to Isabella and me, but how? The thought wouldn't leave me so I tore that page out and tucked it into my purse.

This made me wonder about the status of Isabella's family. Were they U.S. citizens or immigrants "protected" under the Santa Fe's sanctuary policies? Would that cause a problem for Isabella to be here as a visitor? Would she need a vista, or need to apply for a green card? How was this all going to work out? I'd have to check with the agency to find out how they've handled other cases, for I wasn't sure what would be best for her. I berated myself for not having done that already.

Even though I was wound up, I knew I needed sleep, so I changed into my pajamas and climbed into the other queen-sized bed, closed my eyes, and let my mind wander. I didn't think I'd be able to fall asleep so I was happy to wake up eight hours later to face a dancing little girl with Sweet Pea in her arms. Sweet Pea looked like she'd had enough, so I decided to rescue her. "C'mon girls, climb into bed for a hug before we begin our day, okay?" I had to laugh because Sweet Pea's smile in response was wider than Isabella's.

As Isabella settled in next to me, she looked at me with brooding eyes. "Mama?"

"Yes, sweetie, what is it?"

"I don't want to live with anyone else. I don't even know these people you're taking me to, but I don't like them."

"Now, Isabella, how can you say you don't like them until you've met them? That's what we call being prejudiced—when we prejudge someone by making a decision about them before you even meet them. Do you follow what I'm saying?"

"Yes, Mama, but I still don't want to live with them."

"Well, let's just take one step at a time. We're going to meet them tomorrow for a short visit, and we'll see what happens, okay?"

"Okaaay," she answered, doubt in her voice.

"Who wants to take a swim in the hotel pool?"

"I do!" shouted Isabella, pulling on my arm. "C'mon, Mama, let's go!"

Even though I didn't particularly like swimming in a public pool, I was happy to do so for Isabella's sake. She jumped into the shallow end like a pro and bobbed up and down with excitement. She looked at me with pride and said, "Watch what I can do, Mama," and with that, she dunked her whole head underwater. She jumped up quickly, pushing hair out of her eyes, and laughed. "Can you do that?"

I laughed and said, "Not with this hair. We'd never get to Santa Fe!"

Without hesitation, she nodded in agreement, wearing a wide smile.

After we showered and dressed, we nibbled on the freebie breakfast muffin and drank our juice before we dashed back upstairs to get our baggage and check out. We were excited about driving north to Santa Fe to see what awaited us.

J.S. PECK

J oan was reared in a family of readers in small-town Elmira, New York. When she was growing up, each Sunday afternoon was a special time when each member of her family relaxed with a good book. "It is when I began reading the Nancy Drew series that I became intrigued by mysteries. To me, the fun of reading mystery books is to become so involved with the story it  becomes impossible to put the book down. Many times, a good mystery has caused me to stay up all night to finish it to see whether I'm able to figure out whodunit. For anyone who is hooked on reading mystery books, there's nothing better than that."

In addition, Joan was raised to be open-minded and came to the understanding that we are all connected energetically and are able to communicate with others who have passed on. She brings that idea into her Death Card series by having the spirit of Rosie's grandmother pop into her life with advice or loving messages. Rosie herself is portrayed as a psychic, which means she has visions of what is yet to come.

Joan also writes books under the name Joan S. Peck, and that website is www.JoanSPeck.com.

I hope you enjoy reading this book and the entire Death Card series. If you did, please help other readers discover it by leaving a review on Amazon.com. I thank you for your kindness.

—Joan

ACKNOWLEDGMENTS

Many thanks to all those in my family and others who have supported me on my journey to writing mysteries. It's heartwarming to have your encouragement.

From the bottom of my heart, I thank all of you who picked up this book to read. I hope you find enjoyment in every chapter and, even more so, find this book difficult to put down. That's what a good mystery is all about.

To all you readers, I can't thank you enough for taking time to plough through the first version of the book. My appreciation to Doreen Ping, Donna Stidman, Ann Frazier, Sharon Caldwell, Anne Heim, and Rick Purvines.

What makes a good book great? Editing. So with great appreciation for their talent, I thank Shelly Peck, Judi Moreo, and my editor extraordinaire, Meredith Reed. Kudos and gratitude to you all.

I was blessed the day I contacted Kelly Martin to be my book cover designer. Thank you, Kelly, for your creativity and artistic talents. I love your work.

Thank you, Jake Naylor, for designing my website, being my layout person, and so much more. You're a marvel, and you're the best.

BOOKS BY J.S. PECK

THE DEATH CARD SERIES
- Book 1: Death on the Strip
- Book 2: Death at the Lake
- Book 3: Death Returns (November 2018)
- Book 4: Death Waits (February 2019)

BOOKS BY JOAN S. PECK

- *The Seven Major Chakras – Keeping it Simple*
- *A Simple Approach to Living a Successful Life*
- *What You Need to Know to Live a Spiritual Life*
- *Prime Threat – Shattering the Power of Addiction*

Made in the USA
Middletown, DE
15 September 2018